LANDSLIDE!

A new sound reached Nate's ears. A sound he couldn't quite identify. Since it was faint he leaped to the conclusion it must come from a long way off. But then he realized the sound was much closer than he thought but was being smothered by the deluge. He cocked his head, trying to pinpoint where it came from.

"Husband!" Winona cried. She had turned. One arm was upraised, and she was pointing.

Nate looked over his shoulder. He thought for a second he must be seeing things, that it was a trick of the rain and the dark and the wind. But it was no trick, and an icy chill gripped him clear down to his marrow.

The side of the bluff was breaking away. Loosened by the downpour, tons of earth and rock were peeling loose, like the peel of an apple being peeled by a knife. An enormous slide had started.

A slide that was coming down right on top of them!

The *Wilderness* series:

#1: KING OF THE MOUNTAIN
#2: LURE OF THE WILD
#3: SAVAGE RENDEZVOUS
#4: BLOOD FURY
#5: TOMAHAWK REVENGE
#6: BLACK POWDER JUSTICE
#7: VENGEANCE TRAIL
#8: DEATH HUNT
#9: MOUNTAIN DEVIL
#10: BLACKFOOT MASSACRE
#11: NORTHWEST PASSAGE
#12: APACHE BLOOD
#13: MOUNTAIN MANHUNT
#14: TENDERFOOT
#15: WINTERKILL
#16: BLOOD TRUCE
#17: TRAPPER'S BLOOD
#18: MOUNTAIN CAT
#19: IRON WARRIOR
#20: WOLF PACK
#21: BLACK POWDER
#22: TRAIL'S END
#23: THE LOST VALLEY
#24: MOUNTAIN MADNESS
#25: FRONTIER MAYHEM
#26: BLOOD FEUD
#27: GOLD RAGE
#28: THE QUEST
#29: MOUNTAIN NIGHTMARE
#30: SAVAGES
#31: BLOOD KIN
#32: THE WESTWARD TIDE
#33: FANG AND CLAW
#34: TRACKDOWN
#35: FRONTIER FURY
#36: THE TEMPEST
#37: PERILS OF THE WIND
#38: MOUNTAIN MAN
#39: FIREWATER
#40: SCAR
#41: BY DUTY BOUND

#42
WILDERNESS

FLAMES OF JUSTICE

David Thompson

LEISURE BOOKS   **NEW YORK CITY**

A LEISURE BOOK®

April 2004

Published by

Dorchester Publishing Co., Inc.
200 Madison Avenue
New York, NY 10016

ISBN 0-8439-5254-7

The name "Leisure Books" and the stylized "L" with design are trademarks of Dorchester Publishing Co., Inc.

Printed in the United States of America.

Visit us on the web at www.dorchesterpub.com.

#42

WILDERNESS

FLAMES OF JUSTICE

Chapter One

They came out of the west, riding hard—three men, two women and a girl, caked with the dust of many miles.

Martha Barker happened to be outside fetching wood for the cookstove and heard them come up the trail that wound along the Platte River. At the sight of them she tensed. One of the men and both of the women were Indians, and ever since the Sioux counted coup on her brother, Martha had little love for their kind. Quickly, she hurried inside to tell her husband.

The riders saw the log building, and slowed. The two white men glanced at each other. Grinning, the older of the pair quoted from the works of a playwright he admired, "What is this castle called that stands hard by?"

"You can read," the younger man said with a curt nod at a crudely painted sign over the front door: BARKER'S

TRADING POST. In smaller print underneath was the claim, IF YOU NEED IT, WE GOT IT.

"I'll talk to you when you are better tempered to attend," the white-haired man answered, indulging in another quote.

The younger of the two women brought her mare up next to the younger man's bay and said in flawless English, "We should stop, husband. We need to rest." Raven hair hung past her shoulders, framing a face many would call lovely. She wore a beaded buckskin dress and moccasins and had a wide leather belt around her waist. Wedged under it were a pair of flintlocks.

"Every minute costs us, Winona," Nate King said, and gazed longingly to the east. They were pushing as hard as they could but it was nowhere near fast enough to suit him. Like his Shoshone wife, he wore buckskins. He was also armed with a brace of pistols, as well as a Bowie knife, a tomahawk, and a Hawken rifle. Slanted across his broad chest were a possibles bag and an ammo pouch.

"I know. But we should stop just the same." Winona King looked at the older man for support. "Don't you agree?"

Shakespeare McNair pushed his beaver hat back on his head. "It won't do us any good to ride our horses into the ground, that's for sure."

"Or ourselves," said the second woman. She was McNair's wife, Blue Water Woman.

"Please, Pa," threw in the girl. Of them all, Evelyn King showed the most fatigue from weeks spent in the saddle.

That left the last member of their party, a giant Shoshone warrior. He showed his sentiments by sliding off his paint and leading it to a hitch rail where three other horses were already tied.

"See?" Shakespeare said. "Touch The Clouds agrees."

"It's not his son," Nate said.

"Be not lost so poorly in your thoughts," Shakespeare again quoted. "You're being unfair, Horatio. We all care for your boy as if he were our own."

"It's just that—" Nate began, and fell silent. They knew what was at stake as well as he did. He stared at his daughter's weary face. "We can spare an hour, no more."

Tobacco smoke hung thick in the gloom of the ill-lit interior. There was only one window and it was covered with burlap. Light came from two lanterns on pegs on the walls. Mixed with the acrid scent of the smoke were other, less pleasant odors. Trade goods were piled haphazardly on one side of the room, on the other were several tables and a long plank counter.

Nate's green eyes flicked from three grimy characters seated at a table to the keg-bellied proprietor behind the counter. He noticed a mousey woman over in a corner nervously wringing her hands. "We'd like something to wash down the dust."

The man with the big belly rubbed a pudgy hand across stubble that dotted his chin. "We don't serve their kind."

Nate did not have to ask what he meant. He started to bring his Hawken up but Shakespeare gripped his arm, shook his head, and grinned at the bigot.

"Mr. Barker, I presume?"

"What of it?"

"You don't serve females?" Shakespeare asked. "I admire your courage, friend, if not your judgment. Riling the opposite gender is like baiting a griz. You're liable to be clawed to pieces."

"What are you talkin' about, you old coot?" Barker demanded. "I meant we don't serve Injuns."

"Oh. Indians. Of course." Shakespeare's grin widened. "I will not excuse you, you shall not be excused, excuses shall not be admitted, there is no excuse shall serve, you shall not be excused."

"What the hell are you babblin' about?"

"That was the Bard. Old William S., as I like to call him. From *Henry the Fourth*." Shakespeare paused. "Here's another. Thou art a very ragged wart."

"What?"

"A drayman, a porter, a very camel."

"Make sense, damn it."

Shakespeare nodded. "What do you think I have been doing?" He quoted again, "I do care for something, but in my conscience, sir, I do not care for you. If that be to care for nothing, sir, I would it would make you invisible." And with that, McNair smashed the stock of his rifle against Barker's temple and Barker folded at the knees and sprawled in a heap.

Martha Barker cried out and ran to her husband. "You had no call to do that!"

The men at the corner table started to rise but Nate, Winona and Blue Water Woman covered them.

Of all those present, only Touch The Clouds was unaffected. He stood with his huge arms folded, as impassive as a cliff.

As for Shakespeare, he hopped onto the counter and swung his legs over the other side. "I can't abide poor manners, madam. Your husband should learn to control his tongue." Hopping down, he reached for Barker but Martha slapped his calloused hand.

"I don't need your help, Injun lover."

Ignoring her, Shakespeare slid his arm around her husband and hauled him off the floor and around the end of the counter to an empty chair. "What a mountain of mad flesh this rascal is. Fetch water, madam, and hastily, if you please."

From a bucket at the far end of the counter Martha brought a ladle filled to the brim. Shakespeare took it, smiled sweetly, and threw the water in her portly husband's face.

Barker's eyes snapped open and he looked around in confusion before his gaze settled on McNair. "You! You struck me!" He pressed a hand to a welt on his temple. "My head is fit to split!"

"Would that a pumpkin contained half as many seeds." Shakespeare patted Barker's shoulder. "The throbbing will go away. In the meantime, be a gracious host and serve me and my companions."

"The gall!" Barker blustered. "Tellin' a man what he can and can't do in his own place!"

Shakespeare leaned down. "Methinks thou art a general offense and every man should beat thee." He touched a finger to Barker's chin. "Listen closely. We've traveled clear from the Rockies. We're tired and hungry and my patience isn't what it should be. Although yellow teeth aren't anything to brag about, I did you the courtesy of sparing yours. So how about if you return the favor?"

"You're insane," was Barker's opinion.

"Which, if true, would be even more cause not to trifle with me." Shakespeare motioned. "Coffee for us men and tea for the ladies, and juice, if you have any, for little Evelyn there."

Barker glared at McNair, then at Nate, then suddenly rose. "All right. But you'd better have the money to pay for it. I don't give credit."

"Nor would I expect you to." Shakespeare fished in his possibles bag and produced a small pouch. Untying the drawstring, he upended it over his palm and out rolled several glittering yellow rocks.

"What are those?"

"Gold nuggets." Shakespeare selected the smallest, about the size of a marble, and gave it to Barker. "This should cover our expenses, and then some."

Barker held the nugget in the lantern light. "How do I know it's the genuine article? It could be fool's gold."

"The irony would be fitting," Shakespeare said. "But all you need do is bite it to confirm I'm as good as my word."

Gingerly, Barker bit the nugget with his front teeth and examined the indentations. "Land sakes! Real gold! Where did you get these?"

"From one of the dwarves who live high up in the Rockies. I caught him trying to steal carrots out of our garden and he agreed to a swap." Shakespeare lowered his voice. "The Indians say the dwarves live in a city of gold, deep in a cave, and only come out to steal food and collect pinecones."

"You're joshin'."

"I'm joshing," Shakespeare confessed. "I'm also hungry. Any chance we can get some food before we keel over from starvation?"

Barker showed nearly all of his yellow teeth. "Mister,

anything you want, you just ask. My missus and me will wait on you hand and foot. And I'm plumb sorry about our little misunderstandin'."

"Was that plumb or plump?" Shakespeare asked, and shook his head. "Never mind. The important thing is that the fount of brotherly love is once again flowing to the betterment of all."

Touch The Clouds moved over near the wall while the Kings and the McNairs took seats at the table near the door. The three men at the other table had relaxed now that the dispute was over and were engrossed in a game of cards.

Nate King leaned his Hawken against his leg. "I thought you handled that quite well."

Shakespeare chuckled. "Praise him that got thee, she that gave thee suck. Famed be thy tutor, and thy parts of nature thrice-famed beyond." His good humor melted like snow under a blazing sun when he saw the look his wife gave him. "I take it, heart of my heart, you disapprove?"

"You cannot go around bashing everyone who insults you," Blue Water Woman said.

McNair winked at Nate's daughter, Evelyn. "Now you know why her people are called Flatheads. The whole tribe is so level-headed, they never lose their tempers."

The girl giggled. "Uncle Shakespeare, you sure are funny sometimes."

"He is hilarious," Blue Water Woman said.

"What I would like to know," Winona interjected, "is how long it will take us to reach Fort Leavenworth."

"Another week to ten days," Nate guessed. And that was only if their horses didn't give out.

"I still can't believe all that's happened, Pa," Evelyn

said. "I always thought we lived so far from anywhere that the rest of the world would pretty much leave us be."

So had Nate. One of the reasons he chose to live in the Rockies was his dislike of the laws and rules that shackled the common man with invisible chains. Growing up in New York, he had seen how people were made to live as the politicians and others wanted them to. Civilization, he had long ago decided, was a subtle form of slavery, made all the worse because the majority of those under its thumb didn't realize they were enslaved.

Nate preferred the untamed wilderness. He preferred to live where there were no laws or rules other than those a man imposed on himself. Where freedom was a way of life, not an elusive dream. He had grown to treasure it as most men treasured gold, and he took great pride in not answering to anyone, a trait he had instilled in his children. Never in his wildest imaginings had he thought it would reap the bitter harvest that it had.

"The problem with the world, Evelyn," Shakespeare was saying, "is that it has a habit of sticking its big nose into our affairs whether we want it to or not. If the government had left well enough alone, we wouldn't be sitting here."

"Those soldiers were only doing their duty," Winona said.

Her words drew a sharp glance from Nate. "I don't believe my ears. They hunted down our son like we would hunt down a rabid wolf."

"I am only trying to see both sides, husband."

"The only side that counts is *our* side. Our own flesh and blood is at risk and we owe it to him to do all in our power to save him."

"What if the only way to do that is to kill?" Winona asked.

"Whatever it takes," Nate declared.

Now it was Winona who bestowed a sharp glance. "You must not let your love get the better of your reason. That is what he did, and look at where it has got him."

"Nitpick all you want," Nate responded. "But don't expect me to stand by and do nothing when it's our son we're talking about. As an old saying goes, blood is thicker than water."

"Too much blood has already been spilled. Spilling more will not help us." Winona covered his big hands with hers. "Please, husband. Surely there must be a better way."

In the strained silence that fell between them, Shakespeare commented, "There's only one other way that I can think of and there's no guarantee it will work. But I agree with you, Winona. We shouldn't resort to violence except as a last resort."

Nate couldn't deny the logic in their argument. But the whirlwind of emotion that gripped him every time he thought about their son's plight set his blood to boiling. No father worthy of the name would let one of his children come to harm.

Barker came over bearing a wooden tray lined with steaming cups of coffee and tea and a glass of apple cider. "My wife would have brought these herself but she doesn't cotton to redskins much."

"If they love they know not why, they hate upon no better a ground," Shakespeare quoted.

"Don't start with your fancy words again," Barker said. "I was just lettin' you know, is all." He wiped at his sweaty forehead with a sweaty forearm. "Did I hear rightly? You folks are bound for Fort Leavenworth?"

"What of it?" Nate responded.

"Oh, nothin'. It's just that we might be headin' that way ourselves in a month or so," Barker revealed. "Word is, they'll be holdin' the first public hangin' in those parts, and we wouldn't want to miss it."

"Who, pray tell, are they fixing to hang?" Shakespeare inquired.

"Some renegade by the name of Zach King."

Chapter Two

Stanley P. Dagget trudged along the street to his office. He was in no particular hurry to get there. Why should he be, when he could count on one hand the number of times prospective clients had showed up on his doorstep over the past month? Only one of them had actually retained his services. The rest merely wanted advice, which he always offered without charge.

Some of his colleagues poked fun at Stanley about that. He had a lot invested in his career, they reminded him. So it was only fair to require that clients pay for advice as well as other legal services.

Arthur Hunnicut III had suggested that Stanley do as he did and charge by the hour, but to Stanley that smacked of greed. He couldn't in good conscience have charged the elderly widow who came to see him about the pathetic mess in which her husband had left their finances. Or the young couple who only wanted to learn the steps necessary to make out a will.

Arthur had laughed and clapped Stanley on the back. "Do as you please. But I thought your goal in life was to earn a living, not run a charity."

That was Arthur for you, Stanley thought. Always teasing.

He came to the butcher shop and saw his reflection in the window and stopped. He was not much to look at. His nose was too big, for one thing. For another, he was much too short and much too thin. Eating one meal a day wasn't healthy but he couldn't afford to eat more often, not if he was to have enough on hand to pay his monthly rent.

Stanley ran a hand over his threadbare jacket. His clothes were as thin as he was. He would give anything to be able to buy new ones.

He told himself, as he did at least ten times a day, that sooner or later his hard times would end. Sooner or later he would have more clients. Wyandot City was growing, despite the situation with the Indians. Maybe not as fast as the nearby town of Kansas, but that was bound to change, too, once people realized Wyandot City was a nice, quiet, stable community.

Stanley continued to his office and unlocked the door. He stared for a moment at his sign: STANLEY P. DAGGET, ATTORNEY-AT-LAW, and debated whether he should have a larger one made to attract more attention. But it would cost twenty-five cents, twenty-five cents he didn't have.

Removing his hat, Stanley hung it on the hat stand and moved around his old pine desk. His chair creaked as he sat down and he made sure not to rest his left arm on the cracked chair arm for fear it might break. Leaning back, he closed his eyes and considered taking a nap. He was tired. So very tired. Not in body, since he always went to bed punctually at nine o'clock. No, he was tired deeper down, in the core of his being. Tired of the struggle. Tired of being a laughingstock among his peers. Just sick and tired of the whole farce.

Boots clomped on the boardwalk but Stanley didn't think much of it. Passerby on his way elsewhere, he imagined. Then there was a loud knock and the door rattled and Stanley opened his eyes and couldn't move or speak, the shock was so great.

Three men were entering. In the lead was Judge Warren Hardesty, whose ample girth was as talked about as the harshness of the sentences he dispensed so coldly from the bench. There was a joke among the legal community to the effect that if ever a man had a fitting name, Hardesty was the one.

The judge claimed the only other chair without being asked and without offering to shake Stanley's hand in greeting.

The other two were military men. Stanley had never been in the army and didn't know much about insignia and such, but he knew enough to know these were officers and that the ramrod-straight gray-haired man with the hawkish countenance was an officer of considerable rank.

"Good morning, Dagget," Judge Hardesty boomed in that rumbling voice of his. "How have you been?"

Stanley's vocal cords seemed to have taken the stage to St. Louis. He tried to reply and had to swallow twice before he blurted, "Fine, sir. Just fine. To what do I owe the honor of this unusual occurrence?"

"I've come to do you a favor," Judge Hardesty proclaimed.

"Me, sir?" Stanley was amazed Hardesty had remembered he existed. The few times he had appeared in Hardesty's court, the judge treated him as if he had leprosy. He figured it was because Hardesty had to be impartial to administer justice fairly, although he'd noticed that the judge was on extremely friendly terms with some of the more successful attorneys.

"Why do you sound so surprised, Dagget? Just because we don't attend the same club doesn't mean I haven't noticed you. To be quite frank, you're a man after my own heart."

Stanley could not have been more dumbfounded if the sky had opened up and legions of angels descended.

"You're a good man, Dagget. You keep your nose to the grindstone. You don't drink, you don't swear, you don't fritter away your finances on the many and sundry vices to which humankind is susceptible. Quite exceptional, actually."

All that was true, but for the life of him, Stanley didn't feel exceptional.

"So when the government requested my advice in a certain crucial matter, naturally you were the one I thought of."

"Are you sure you have the right man, sir?" It came out before Stanley could stop himself. He was sure they could see his ears were red because he could feel them burn, as they always did when he was embarrassed.

"Quite the little jester, aren't you?" Judge Hardesty reached into a pocket and took out a cigar. He lit it with a flourish and let out a cloud of smoke before saying,

"Now then, to business, shall we? How would you like to have more clients than you can handle?"

Stanley fought down an urge to pinch himself.

"All it would take, Dagget, is one case. A case that puts you in the public eye. A case that will have your name on the lips of every man and woman in the territory. In the country, even."

"The whole country?" Stanley said incredulously.

"Bear with me, boy," Judge Hardesty said, and exhaled another cloud of smoke. "First, let me introduce my associates. This distinguished gentleman to my right is General Risher. He's come all the way from Washington to oversee the matter we will shortly discuss."

"Pleased to meet you, sir."

General Risher smiled thinly. "Mr. Dagget. I have heard a lot about you."

Stanley almost said, "You have?"

The judge nodded at the other officer. "And this is Lieutenant Pickforth from Fort Leavenworth. He's temporarily been assigned as the general's adjutant."

"Please to meet you, too, Lieutenant," Stanley offered, and wondered why it was that Pickforth's name was vaguely familiar.

"Now then"—Judge Hardesty blew a smoke ring—"how would you like that case I was talking about handed to you on a silver platter?"

"Who do I have to shoot?" Stanley joked. Not that he ever would. He didn't own a gun and never had, and couldn't even bring himself to harm the mouse that regularly raided his pantry.

Hardesty laughed and the officers grinned but Stanley had the impression they were only being polite.

"The beauty of this arrangement is that all you have to do is agree to take the case and it's yours. Keep in mind that if you refuse, we can find any number of attorneys willing to leap at the chance."

"Tell me more," Stanley said eagerly.

"You've heard of the renegade, I take it?"

"Zach King?" Stanley nodded. Who hadn't? When King was brought in, the story made the front page. A trading post had been wiped out, all the traders slain and the post burned to the ground by a war party King allegedly led. "A most dreadful incident," Stanley commented.

It was General Risher who responded. "We want it to be an instructive incident, Mr. Dagget."

"I'm afraid I don't follow you, sir."

For some reason the general winked at the judge. "Need I point out that the frontier is a hotbed of violence? Hostile tribes constantly make life difficult for settlers and the army. Riffraff like this Zach King are all too common and make matters vastly worse. The army wants to make an object lesson of him."

"After he is duly found guilty, of course?"

Judge Hardesty chortled and glanced at the general. "What did I tell you? Is he the perfect choice or not?"

Suddenly Stanley divined why they had paid him a visit, and his gut balled into a knot.

"An excellent point, Dagget," the judge said. "Everyone is entitled to due process, even someone like this King. That includes the right to be defended by a competent attorney. But lawyers are as human as everyone else. Most would like to see King hang. My task has been to find one willing to defend him to the best of their ability."

This time Stanley couldn't resist. "And you chose me?"

"Why not? I've already commented on your virtues. And while you don't have a lot of experience, what you lack in that regard you more than make up for with your devotion to principle. You did tell me once, did you not, that the foundation on which the legal profession rests is fairness?"

Stanley had indeed made the comment, back when they first met, and as he recalled, the judge had given him a strange look. "That I did, sir."

"Then surely you feel Zach King deserves the same fair legal treatment as everyone else?"

"Of course he does."

"Will you agree to represent him? Court convenes in three days and you'll need every minute to prepare your case."

"Not so fast," General Risher broke in. "There are a few questions I would like to ask. That is, if Mr. Dagget doesn't mind."

"Go right ahead," Stanley said.

"Is it true you've only been practicing law for ten months?"

"Yes. But that doesn't mean I'm incompetent, if that's what you're implying. I studied law under Benjamin Forwood of Jefferson City. As the judge will confirm, Mr. Forwood has an impeccable reputation."

Judge Hardesty nodded.

"Why move from Jefferson City to here?" General Risher inquired.

It was a question Stanley had been asked before. Many times. Jefferson City was the state capital. Wyandot City was a city only in name and not a tenth as big. It also had the unique distinction of being the only community in Missouri owned by Indians.

That was a story in itself. Decades past, the area was designated a reservation for the Delawares. But about six years ago another tribe came on the scene: the Wyandots from Ohio, a shrewd and industrious people who had adopted white ways. They bought the land from the Delawares and laid out their own city, including a school and a church. To help their new community thrive, they invited whites to settle among them, but so far few had taken them up on the offer.

Stanley was one of those few. As a result, he was forever being teased by his peers in Kansas, which some were calling Kansas City although it wasn't officially chartered as a city yet.

"The bar at Jefferson City is quite crowded," Stanley now enlightened the general. "A few of the more prominent lawyers get the lion's share of the business and the rest are reduced to jostling for scraps."

"I see. But why not go to a bigger city like New Orleans or Chicago?" Risher asked. "Why here, of all places?"

Stanley gave his patented answer. "Everyone has to start somewhere and Wyandot City is as good a place as any."

"You don't mind living among Indians?"

"Why should I? The Wyandots are human beings, aren't they? When you get right down to it, they're no different than us. They wear white clothes, they live as whites do." Stanley paused. "What does this have to do with anything?"

"I merely wanted to learn your stance in regard to Indians," General Risher clarified. "You will, after all, be representing a man accused of perpetrating heinous atrocities in collusion with Indians."

"Ah," Stanley said. "The color of a man's skin is of no consequence to me whatsoever."

"Then you agree to be Zach King's defense attorney?" Judge Hardesty pressed him.

Stanley was immensely flattered that he was the first one the judge had thought of. The case could be the godsend he was hoping for. "Yes, sir, I wholeheartedly agree."

Judge Hardesty beamed. "Marvelous. Simply marvelous. We'll inform Colonel Templeton at Fort Leavenworth. You may go visit your new client tomorrow, if you wish. Be assured that all depositions and transcripts to date will be turned over to you so you may study them."

"You've thought of everything," Stanley complimented him.

"I try, Dagget," Judge Hardesty said. "I truly try." Puffing on his cigar, he raised his ponderous bulk from the chair. "If you have any questions, talk to General Risher. From this moment on, you and I should have as little contact as possible."

"Why is that, your honor?"

"Didn't I tell you? I'm presiding at the trial. We must be sure not to present the impression of impropriety." The judge turned to go. "I can't discuss the case with the prosecuting attorney, either."

"Do you happen to know who that will be?"

"Arthur Hunnicut."

Stanley's sense that fortune was smiling on him withered on the vine. "Arthur? He's never lost a case."

"Hasn't he? It's neither here nor there. Your only concern should be saving Zach King from the gallows."

"I'll do my best," Stanley vowed.

Judge Hardesty grinned. "That's what we're counting on."

Chapter Three

It was the middle of the morning when Touch The Clouds told Nate King they were being followed.

"Are you certain?" Nate asked in the Shoshone tongue. The trail they were using saw steady use. It was one of the main east-west arteries across the plains, and it wasn't uncommon to come across travelers bound in either direction.

The giant warrior pointed a finger as thick as a metal spike. "Twice I have seen three white men. Always the same three, and always the same distance back."

"It could be they are in as big a hurry as we are," Nate speculated.

"There were three whites at the trading post," Touch The Clouds said.

"So?"

"They saw Carcajou's gold."

Preoccupied as he was with worry for his son, Nate hadn't thought much about the difficulty at Barker's. It had been a trifling affair as frontier affairs went. But he did recollect the three shabbily clad men with their unkempt beards and tangled manes of hair, over at the other table. Twisting in the saddle, he scanned the belt of vegetation bordering the shallow, sluggish Platte. Other than a jay high in a tree and a pair of ducks out on the river, the woodland was still and peaceful.

"I can wait for them," Touch The Clouds said.

"No," Nate said. "If you were to kill one or two and word got out, you would be hunted down like my son." It was an unfair fact of life that while whites didn't mind that much when a white man killed another white, they minded a lot when a red man was to blame. "I'll take care of it."

They rode until the sun was directly overhead. Nate called a halt in a clearing near the river, and after the horses were watered and the women and his daughter were at ease in the shade of a maple tree, he went to where McNair stood on a high bank watching bass swim just below the surface.

"How now, my Lord of Worcester," Shakespeare quoted. "Too bad we can't spend the afternoon here. I could go for a pan of fried fish smothered in butter." He smirked. "Provided we had butter."

"I'm staying behind when you and the others go on."

Shakespeare's brow knit. "Is there something I should know, Horatio? Trouble, perchance?"

Nate told him about the trio shadowing them.

"If this were true, then should I know this secret," said Shakespeare, reciting the Bard. "You'll need someone to watch your back."

"One of us should stay with the women. Just in case."

"Our lady loves are perfectly capable of taking care of themselves."

"In the wilderness, yes, I'll grant you," Nate acknowledged. "But it's the white world we're about to enter."

"Very well. I'll do it but I'll do it under protest. Should you go and get yourself rubbed out, I'll bury you next to a tree and carve your epitaph in the trunk." Shakespeare adopted a formal tone. "Here lies Nathaniel King, laid low in the prime of manhood by his own pigheadedness."

Nate refrained from telling Winona until everyone was mounted and ready to ride on.

"Why didn't you tell me this sooner, husband?" she asked accusingly. "I will stay with you."

"And what of our daughter?" Nate said, with a bob of his chin at Evelyn, who was watching a yellow butterfly flit among blue and purple flowers.

"Blue Water Woman and Shakespeare will look after her, if it comes to that." Winona started to slide her leg off the mare but he held it, preventing her from climbing down.

"Would you leave her alone in the world, wife? A girl of her tender years?"

"You are my man. My place is at your side."

"Any other time I would agree. But one of us must reach our son." Nate squeezed her leg. "Please."

"Very well. But if they kill you, I will kill them." Winona clucked to the mare and reluctantly headed out.

"You're not coming, Pa?" Evelyn said.

"I'll catch up in a bit," Nate promised. He smiled and watched until they were out of sight, then quickly led his bay into the undergrowth and moved to a broad oak beside the trail.

Soon birds were chirping, and over at the river three doe ventured out of the brush to drink.

Nate peered westward, waiting with the patience of a

mountain lion for his prey to appear. He hoped Touch
The Clouds was wrong. Trouble like this so close to the
fort was trouble he didn't need. He thought of Zach, lan-
guishing in the army stockade, according to Barker at the
trading post. *How had it come to this?* he asked himself.
How had everything that had once been so right gone so
terribly wrong?

Movement drew Nate's attention to a bend to the west.
Into view trotted the threesome, riding abreast. They were
talking and joking, but their smiles died when he strode
to the middle of the trail and planted himself with his
Hawken leveled. "That's far enough."

Weasels in human garb, they were stamped from the
same crude mold. They all had slick, greasy hair, greasy
faces, and beady eyes that gleamed with all the lower
instincts to which men were prone. The greasiest, the one
in the middle, leaned on his saddle and quirked his mouth
in what he probably thought was an innocent smile.

"What's the meanin' of this, mister? You can't go
around pointin' a rifle at folks like that without a reason."

"Give it up," Nate said.

"Give what up?" The spokesman continued his sham.
"We're on our way to St. Louis to spend a month or so
whorin' and guzzlin' bug juice."

"Out of our way, big man," barked the weasel on the
left.

"It won't wash." Nate had his thumb on the Hawken's
hammer, his forefinger on the trigger. "Shuck your artil-
lery and climb off. I'm taking your horses."

"The hell you say!" growled the man in the middle. "If
you think you're strandin' us afoot in the middle of creation, you've got another think comin'. We're peaceable

coons mindin' our own business and you'd be wise to do the same."

"What you are," Nate said harshly, "are vermin who want to get their hands on my friend's poke. You're hoping to jump us some night soon but the only jumping you'll be doing is down off those nags."

"Like hell," said the rider on the right. "Who do you think you are, anyhow?"

"This is a free country, mister," the man in the middle flared. "And we can do as we damn well please. Now move or prepare to meet your maker!"

The weasel on the left was fidgeting in his saddle like he had red ants crawling up his britches, so Nate wasn't surprised when he whipped a rifle to his shoulder to take aim. Nate fired from the hip. The Hawken boomed, belching smoke and lead, and the rider was catapulted off his mount and tumbled in the dirt with a loud thud. Instantly, Nate grabbed a pistol from his belt but the other two broke to either side and were spurring their horses for cover. He took a bead just as vegetation swallowed them, and had to hold his fire.

The man who had been shot was still alive. Roaring like an enraged bear, he heaved to his knees with a pistol in each hand and snapped off a shot that buzzed like an angry hornet past Nate's ear.

Backpedaling toward the oak, Nate fired and saw blood burst in a fine spray from the man's shoulder. The man went down, and Nate ducked behind the tree to reload his spent weapons.

An unnatural stillness claimed the woods.

Nate opened his ammo pouch and was reaching into it when some brush forty feet away rustled and a rifle barrel poked out. He ducked and darted to one side just as the rifle discharged. The slug intended for his chest struck the tree. He kept going, zigzagging until he came to a thicket. Hunkering, his fingers flying, he reloaded.

Nate tried not to make noise but when he was shoving the ball and patch down, the ramrod scraped the barrel. The sound wasn't that loud but it convinced him to change position.

On cat's feet Nate glided from cover to cover until he was near the trail once again. The man he had shot was gone. Either the cutthroat's friends had dragged him off or there was enough life left in him for him to move under his own power.

Scanning the vegetation, Nate waited for one of them to make a mistake. He tried not to let his mind wander. Tried not to think of his son and the burning anxiety that had gnawed at his insides for weeks now. But it was hard not to, even at a time like this. Every parent's worst nightmare was the loss of a child. Of all life's injustices, it reigned supreme. The notion of possibly losing Zach made him want to scream his fury to the wind.

Weeds moved off to Nate's left, and a greasy face appeared. He couldn't tell which one it was. Careful not to give himself away, he trained his Hawken on the center of the face and was about to squeeze the trigger when the weeds closed and the face disappeared.

Nate frowned. He had been a shade too slow. Caution was commendable but he must take his shots when he got the chance. He lowered his rifle, then spotted a different face staring at him from behind a tree. The man was taking aim.

Nate rolled a split-second before the blast and felt a

tug on his sleeve. Heaving erect behind a tree, he listened for the crackle of brush or the crunch of leaves, for anything that would give him a clue to where the three were. But they were backwoods savvy, these three, and knew better than to give themselves away.

Suddenly, and much to Nate's surprise, one of them gave a shout.

"You there! Mountain man!"

Nate wasn't foolhardy enough to answer and let them know where he was.

"You hurt Caleb something awful. He's got two of your bullets in him and is bleedin' like a stuck piglet."

As best Nate could tell, the man was twenty-five to thirty yards to the southwest in the high weeds.

"Caleb needs tendin' and he needs it quick. How about you let us be and go your way in peace if we give you our word that we'll forget all about your gabby friend and his gold?"

Nate longed for a target. For the sight of a shoulder or an arm, anything.

"Be reasonable, damn it! Caleb is my brother and I don't want him dyin'. What do you say?"

Can I trust them? Nate asked himself. The man sounded sincere but if there was one lesson his perilous life on the frontier had taught him, it was that a too-trusting nature led to a too-early grave.

"Damn your hide!" the man fumed. "If that's how you want to be, fine! Never let it be said the Ketchum brothers can't hold their own."

After that the forest was as still as a cemetery. Nate's thumb on the Hawken's hammer became cramped, he held it there so long. He thought he saw something move and glanced to his left but it was only a bumblebee going about its daily business of drinking nectar. He glanced to his right and was nearly startled out of his skin. "Get down! They'll see you!"

Touch The Clouds had materialized out of nowhere. Calmly cradling his rifle in his huge arms, he said, "They are gone, Grizzly Killer."

"Are you sure?" Nate regretted the question the moment it passed his lips. It was an inadvertent insult but his wife's cousin overlooked the slur.

"I found their tracks leading west to where they climbed on their horses and rode away."

"Why are you here?" Nate asked, annoyed at himself for letting the trio slip off. It was a mistake only a rank amateur would make.

"Winona sent me. She and Blue Flower were worried."

Blue Flower was Evelyn's Shoshone name. Nate cradled his own rifle and said testily, "I can take care of myself, thank you."

Touch The Clouds's dark eyes narrowed. "What is the real reason you are upset with me?"

"Your testimony is crucial to saving Zach," Nate answered. "If anything were to happen to you—"

"Do you think the whites will believe me? Most I have met think anyone who is not white speaks with two tongues."

"They'll believe you," Nate said, but even to his own ears, he lacked conviction. "Once they know the full story, they'll let him go."

"The soldiers they sent were told the full story," Touch The Clouds noted, "but they—" The giant paused. "What is it whites call what they did? There is no word for it in the tongue of my people."

"Arrested," Nate said in English. "They took him into custody." He switched to Shoshone. "Whites take those who do not live by their rules and put them in a cage made of metal bars." There was no word in the Shoshone language for "jail," either.

"Whites have strange ways."

Nate could understand why his friend found the idea so foreign. Indian tribes handled things differently. Many had special warrior societies who policed their villages and punished offenders for various infractions. But Indians didn't hold their own captive, or throw a rope around a warrior's neck and string him from the nearest tree or a gallows. The worst they did was banish someone.

"I talked to the leader of the soldiers myself," Touch The Clouds reminded him. "But in his heart he did not accept my words."

"I have not talked to him yet," Nate said.

"Maybe he will believe you since you are white."

Nate doubted it would make a difference, not after what Zach had done. In Nate's estimation the deed was justified, but the army hadn't seen it that way and a judge likely wouldn't, either. "All we can do is hope."

"I am sorry, Grizzly Killer. I should not have let Stalking Coyote talk me into attacking the trading post."

"My son should have known better," Nate said. And there, as Shakespeare might say, was the rub. What in God's name had made his son think he could get away with something like that?

"I hope Stalking Coyote is still alive," Touch The Clouds commented.

"That makes two of us."

Chapter Four

She had cried so many tears that she thought she could not possibly shed another. But each morning they flowed anew, and during the day she cried so long and so hard, by evening her cheeks and chin and neck were wet with the residue of her sorrow and she was emotionally and physically drained.

Louisa King had known sadness in her life. She had lost her mother on the family's trek west, she had lost her father to hostiles. But she had never known sadness like this. Never known sorrow that filled every fiber of her being.

She tried to resist the deluge. She tried to assure herself that everything would work out, that her husband would be found innocent and they would be permitted to return to their cabin high in the distant Rockies. But then the thought of what Zach had done would sear her to her core, and her delusion would die aborning.

Lou was scared. More scared than she ever remembered being. The kind of scared where a person's heart became ice and their soul was frozen in complete and terrible dread.

She could not bear to countenance the thought of losing Zach. He was everything to her. As much a part of her as the breath of life itself. His death would crush her to the point where she would not want to live. Of that she was certain. Even if it meant perishing by her own hand.

Louisa was sprawled on the musty sofa in the small apartment she was renting in the bustling town of Kansas, weeping into the cushions, when there came a rather timid knock at her door. Since she knew no one there, and since the town was home to riffraff of every stripe, Lou took up one of her pistols and demanded, "Who is it and what do you want?"

"Mrs. King? Mrs. Louisa King? I'm here to talk to you about your husband."

"Are you another newspaper reporter?" Lou demanded. "I thought I'd made it plain that I'll shoot the next one of you vultures who shows his face."

"I'm an attorney, Mrs. King. Specifically, I'm your husband's attorney, and we very much need to discuss his case."

Sliding the bolt, Lou snatched at the latch and found herself staring at a short, skinny man in rumpled clothes who didn't look much older than she was. "You claim to be Zach's lawyer?"

The man doffed a bowler. "Stanley P. Dagget, at your service. Yes, I'm to represent Mr. King, and I would like to interview you to get your side of events in explicit detail. As background, you might say."

"I don't understand," Lou said suspiciously. She had cause to be wary. A couple of weeks ago a reporter had tried to trick her into relating details by misleading her into thinking he had been sent by the army to review "the pertinent facts," as the imposter phrased it. Fortunately for her, she had remembered seeing him among the pack of reporters who mobbed her when she first arrived. "We don't have the money to hire a lawyer or I'd have hired one by now."

"We'll discuss my reimbursement later," the attorney said. "For now, I should think you would be pleased I'm willing to take your case. From what I hear, most attorneys don't want anything to do with it. But to prove my credentials are bona fide, here." He opened his valise and took out a sheet of paper. "This is my letter of introduction, signed by General Risher. He assured me that you know who he is."

"We've spoken a few times," Lou admitted. She examined the letter. It was brief and to the point, like the general himself: *This is to inform you that Stanley P. Dagget, Esquire, has agreed to serve as your husband's defense counsel.* "Who asked you to be our lawyer, Mr. Dagget?" she asked. "General Risher?"

"I'm not at liberty to say, but it wasn't him, no." Dagget glanced past her. "Perhaps you could see fit to invite me in?"

"I reckon I'd best hear you out." Lou took her other hand from behind the door. He saw the pistol, and blinked.

"You wouldn't use that, would you?"

"Why not? You wouldn't be the first person I've shot." Lou moved aside so he could enter and inwardly grinned at the glance he gave her flintlock. "But don't worry, Mr. Dagget. I'm not about to make wolf bait of someone who might be able to help my husband."

"You may call me Stanley if you so wish." Dagget sat on the sofa with his knees together and his arms at his sides. "Nice place you have here."

Louisa bolted the door. Since the old sofa and a battered table were the only furniture, she sat crosslegged on the floor. "I can't say I like the idea of a lawyer who tells lies, Stanley."

"I was merely being polite." Dagget looked away and became nearly as red as a tomato.

"Be honest instead." Lou regarded her lodgings with distaste. "This apartment isn't fit for a goat but it's all I can afford."

"The army wouldn't let you stay in the guest quarters at the fort?"

"I'm the wife of a renegade, remember?" Lou gestured. "Colonel Templeton was nice enough, but I wouldn't stay there anyway. I don't want to be anywhere near Lieutenant Pickforth, the officer who brought my husband in."

Dagget snapped his fingers. "Now I know why that name was so familiar. I wish I had known who he was when I met him."

Lou could not say her initial impression of the lawyer was flattering. "Have you talked to Zach?"

"Not yet. I was hoping to do so with you along. I've been told he's extremely belligerent and has attacked his guards several times."

"Only because they've goaded him into it." Once, Lou had arrived at the stockade to find Zach bleeding and bruised from a beating inflicted, Zach said, for no reason at all. When she complained, the sergeant in charge claimed the guards were only defending themselves.

"I'll investigate his treatment when we're out there." Dagget opened his valise and spread out a sheaf of papers. "What I need at the moment is to familiarize myself with the basics of the case. For instance, is it true this all started when your husband led a band of Shoshone warriors in wiping out a trading post?"

Lou hesitated.

"Mrs. King? You criticized me for telling a small fib, so I expect only the most ruthless honesty from you. Did he or did he not lead a war party against the Ham's Fork Trading Post, as it was called?"

"He helped the Shoshones, yes."

"Helped them how? He held their horses for them? He gave them guns? Or did he, in fact, instigate the massacre?"

"Those traders were scum. They were cheating the Shoshones and getting warriors drunk on whiskey. They tried to kill a Shoshone chief who wouldn't let them get away with their shenanigans. Then they had the gall to set another tribe, the Crows, against the Shoshones, trying to stir up a war. Something had to be done."

"Perhaps so. But your husband presumed to take the law into his own hands. Surely you realize how wrong that was?"

"What law?" Lou rebutted. "In the mountains we live as free as the birds and the beasts."

Dagget pursed his lips. "An interesting point, but one the prosecuting attorney would make short shrift of. The fact is, Mrs. King, that while the plains and the Rockies are technically outside the legal jurisdiction of any state or municipality, all the land from the Mississippi River to the Pacific Ocean is still recognized as part of the United States of America and subject to applicable federal laws."

Lou almost rose off the floor. "That's just plain stupid! Hellfire, Stanley, no one out there pays any attention to what's legal and what's not. Do you think the Blackfeet give a good damn that it's against the law to kill? Or the Piegans or the Sioux?"

Dagget changed color again, but only to a slightly pinkish shade. "The prosecution will say they are Indians and do not know any better. Your husband, being part white, should."

"My husband was raised to do right, no matter what, and that's exactly what he did when he rubbed out those stinking, thieving, murdering bastards who were posing as traders."

"You certainly can turn a colorful phrase. I hope you won't resort to such language on the witness stand. It might prejudice the jury."

"Zach might be strung up for what he did and you're worried about me using bad language?"

"Your behavior, Mrs. King, can directly impact the verdict. When you're called to the witness stand, and rest assured you will be, I advise that you present yourself as a lady and not as a"—Dagget stopped and seemed to be searching for the right words—"not as a wilderness wildcat."

Lou had rarely been so offended. "I'll have you know I can be as much a prim and proper lady as the next female."

"Oh? And when was the last time you saw a lady wear buckskins and moccasins? Or have a knife strapped to her hip? Or her hair trimmed so boyishly?"

Lou touched her hair. "My pa cut it short like this to fool folks into thinking I was a boy."

Dagget cocked his head. "Why on earth would a father do a bizarre thing like that?"

"So I wouldn't be raped. We'd heard a lot of tales about hostiles and renegade whites and the like." Lou sighed. "When I was little, I had hair down to my waist. But after

Pa cut it, I grew to like not having it snarled and tangled all the time."

"Well, that's really neither here nor there. The important point is to gain the respect and sympathy of the gentlemen of the jury."

"And I do that by wearing a dress and doing my hair up nice so I'll look respectable?" Louisa snorted. "I thought Zach's trial was about the law, not how pretty I can be."

"Legal niceties are only part of the equation," Dagget said. "Your husband will also be judged by how well he deports himself in the courtroom. Him, and everyone who has anything to do with him."

Lou wanted to stay angry but the lawyer was being so reasonable, she couldn't. "This whole business is more complicated than I thought."

"Not actually, not once you see it for what it is." Dagget reflected a few moments. "A trial is a lot like a play, Mrs. King. Each of the participants, or each of the actors, if you will, must play their part and play it well in order to influence the outcome the way they want." He paused, then stated, "I give you my solemn word I'll do all in my power to have your husband set free."

"Even now that you know he took part in the attack?" Lou said skeptically.

"A client's innocence or guilt is irrelevant," Dagget said. "Lawyers don't serve the letter of the law. They try to bend the law to the best interests of those who hire them." He consulted his papers. "Now then, where were we? Ah, yes. Lieutenant Pickforth alleges that your husband later murdered the brother of the owner of the trading post while the man was in army custody."

"Phineas Borke. He had kidnapped me to use as bait to take revenge on Zach for killing his brother, Artemis."

"But it says here the army rescued you before Phineas was killed."

"Yes."

"And that Lieutenant Pickforth actually had Phineas in custody."

"Yes.

"Yet your husband killed him anyway?"

"Yes."

Dagget stared at her. "Permit me to be frank, Mrs. King. I might, and I stress might, be able to save your husband from the hangman's noose. But it will take a miracle to keep him out of prison."

"You're giving up before we begin?"

"On the contrary. I take my responsibilities seriously. I'm merely doing you the courtesy of letting you know exactly where we stand."

Lou stood and walked to the dusty window. Her hopes, so freshly raised, had been dashed. "My husband wouldn't last a year in prison. He could never stand being denied his freedom."

"You would be surprised at the things people can become accustomed to."

"Can you imagine a wolf in a cage, Stanley? Or a mountain lion? It would be the same with Zach. Prison would eat away at his spirit until there was nothing left." Lou folded her arms across her chest. "In some ways, hanging might be better."

"Which of us is ready to give up now?"

If this lawyer only knew, Lou thought. She would do whatever it took to free her man. That included breaking him out of the stockade, should it come to that, and spending the rest of her life as a fugitive. She would rather live on the run with Zach than spend the rest of her days without him.

"In a few hours I should receive the prosecution's list of witnesses, and I must prepare a similar list for them," Dagget disclosed. "Is there anyone in particular we should place on the stand?"

"I expected my father-in-law and some others to show up long ago," Louisa said, "but something must have happened. I'm beginning to worry they might not make it."

"Do you have any friends here or at the fort? Anyone at all?"

Lou turned. "Just you."

Stanley P. Dagget coughed and shuffled his papers into a neat pile. He put them back in his small valise. "I trust you will accompany me to Fort Leavenworth tomorrow? I'll rent a carriage and be here by ten."

An idea came to her. "Will we be able to talk to Zach in private?"

"That can be arranged, yes."

Louisa's pulse quickened. Here was an unexpected opportunity. Usually the guards watched her like hungry hawks watch a prairie dog and never left the two of them alone. Tomorrow she would try to smuggle in weapons and break out again with Zach at her side. "I can't tell you how much I am looking forward to our visit."

"That's the spirit. Never say die."

"Not me," Lou said, and tingled with excitement.

Chapter Five

He had always hated them. The ones who despised him because he was half-and-half. The ones who looked down their noses at "breeds." Since he was old enough to remember, he had endured their looks and the comments they muttered behind his back. "Pay no attention to them," his father had said. "They're just bigots." Easy for his father to say when his father was not the brunt of their bigotry.

Then came his teen years, and he grew tall and strong. There were not as many looks, not as many comments. But that was only because they did not want to anger him. Everyone "knew" breeds had short tempers. Everyone "knew" how violent breeds were.

He became a man, and he rarely encountered the bigotry anymore. Until now. Until he was brought back in chains and thrown into a filthy cell in the army stockade. Many of the soldiers gave him that look and did not care if he saw them do it. Many made comments and did not care if he heard. They hated him. And he hated them right back.

Zachary King squatted in a far corner of his cell, his bedraggled hair half over his face, and pondered. He had taken about as much as he could stand. The insults were bad enough; the beatings were another matter.

Zach looked down at himself. At the beaded buckskins his wife had made, once so new and beautiful, now as

filthy as his cell. At the shackles on his ankles and his
wrists, at the dry blood caking them. He sniffed, and
scrunched his nose. He smelled like the hind end of a
buffalo. Never in his life had he been so dirty, so foul, so
ashamed.

A metallic rasp from down the narrow hall warned him
that the door at the far end on the right was about to open,
and he looked up as light spiked the gloom. A two-legged
bear with more fat than muscle lumbered past several cells
and stopped at his.

"How are we feelin' today, breed?" Sergeant Rotowski
asked. "Have anything to say to me, do you?" He smacked
the club in his right hand against his left palm, and
smirked.

Zach stared. His right cheek was still split from the last
beating, his lips puffed and cracked. He stared through his
hair and imagined slicing a knife across the pig's throat
and seeing red, warm blood gush.

Sergeant Rotowski laughed. "I didn't think so. Even the
wildest dog will break, you beat it often enough and hard
enough."

Zach imagined placing the muzzle of a rifle to the pig's
face and squeezing the trigger and seeing the pig's brains
splatter all over the far wall.

"You get to go out for exercise today. Colonel's orders.
Were it up to me, I'd leave you here to rot. But they want
you healthy when they hang you, I reckon."

Zach thought how wonderful it would be to take a tomahawk and split the pig's head from forehead to the chin.

"On your feet, breed." Rotwoski took a large ring of
keys from his belt and selected one and opened the door.
"Let's go."

Rising, Zach shuffled over. He had learned how to move without tripping but he could never take full strides, only short, sliding steps. His wrists in front of him, he turned left and hobbled to a metal door. Rotowski shouldered him aside to open it, then gave him a push. He was surprised to find two others there. Normally they exercised him alone.

"Half an hour, breed," the sergeant reiterated, and slammed the door with a loud clang.

Zach squinted in the bright glare of the sun. He moved to one side to be by himself. With his back to the others, he breathed deep of the clean if dusty air. Across the way, cavalry were drilling on the parade ground, which they sometimes did for as much as five or six hours a day. He could see the HQ, as the soldiers referred to their headquarters, and the sutler's.

His eyes adjusted, and Zach gazed at the puffy white clouds floating free and easy overhead. He envied them their freedom, envied them being able to go wherever the wind took them. Of all the torments he had to bear, the loss of his freedom was one of the worst.

The worst was being separated from his wife. Zach missed Lou so much, the mere thought of her filled him with an ache that hurt more than all the beatings and the too-tight shackles combined. He remembered the sweet joy of her arms around his neck and her soft lips on his mouth, and his chest and throat grew congested until it reached the point where he could scarcely breathe.

At night the torment was unending. Zach could not stop thinking about her. He would toss and turn and fight back tears and clench his hands until his nails bit into his palms. He yearned for her as he had never yearned for anything his whole life long. Her visits were the only bright spots in the dull horror of his captivity. They wouldn't let her see him more than three times a week, and only for fifteen precious minutes each time.

"What have we here?"

The gruff query intruded on Zach's wistful longing, jarring him back to the bleak here and now.

"Looks to me like some sort of animal," said another voice that grated like quartz rubbing against quartz.

Zach slowly turned. He had not paid much attention to the two prisoners. Both were soldiers, and both were white. That was not unusual. Soldiers were always getting into trouble for sleeping on duty or being drunk and disorderly or for any of a dozen other infractions. But it was unusual that these two were clean-shaven and had clean uniforms and boots, and that only their wrists were shackled, not their legs.

"Didn't you hear me, boy?" said the second one. "I just called you an animal."

"Maybe the cat's got his tongue," joked the first. "Or maybe he's just yellow, like all breeds."

Zach began to turn away.

"Look at me when I'm talking to you!" the second one declared, and jabbed him in the ribs.

Anger boiled in Zach like water in a stew pot but he held his temper in check and merely glared.

"He's giving us the evil eye, Walt," the first one said, and laughed. "I'm trembling in my boots. How about you?"

"Oh, I'm trembling, all right, Harve," the second one said. "I'm so scared I could wet myself." He started to unbutton his pants.

Zach glanced toward where the guards usually stood but no guards were there. Nor were there any soldiers anywhere within earshot except those over on the parade ground. It dawned on him that something was amiss, that it was no coincidence these two were in the yard with him. He felt drops splatter on his moccasins and looked down.

Walt was pissing on him.

"Give him a shower, why don't you?" Harve gleefully goaded. "Show the breed what we think of worthless trash who go around murdering white folks."

The world seemed to acquire a red haze. Zach felt his temples pound and heard the roar of his blood in his veins. Lunging, he grabbed Walt's penis and twisted. Walt howled and tried to leap back but Zach pulled with all his might and Walt screeched like a ten-year-old girl.

Harve rushed in to help, swinging both his brawny arms like clubs and roaring, "Damn your breed hide!"

Ducking, Zach slammed his wrists against Harve's right kneecap. Metal crunched on bone and Harve yelped and staggered to one side and Zach went after him, swinging again and again at the much bigger man's legs, striking knees and shins and then bringing the shackles down hard on an instep.

Walt was doubled over, clutching himself, his face purple. "I'll pound you to a pulp!" he squeaked.

Zach twisted as Harve clutched for his neck, then whipped his wrists against Harve's chin. He put all he had into the blow and it rocked Harve on his heels. Zach followed it with a looping smash to the head that felled Harve like a poled ox.

"You stinking breed!" Walt raged.

Iron fingers clamped on Zach's shoulders and he was
spun around. He raised his arms to defend himself, thinking Walt would batter him just as he had battered Harve,
but Walt kicked him in the gut. Now he was the one who
bent in half. Out of the corner of his eye he saw Walt
raise both wrists to finish him off. Shackled as he was, he
couldn't move fast enough to evade the swing, so he
didn't try. He stepped in under it and absorbed it on his
upper back while simultaneously slamming his shackles
against Walt's groin.

Tottering as if he were besotted with whiskey, Walt
bleated, "Not there again! Not there again!"

"Enough of this!"

Zach turned. Harve was on his knees and was unbut-
toning his shirt. The reason became clear when Harve's
hand slipped underneath and reappeared holding a long-
bladed knife.

"Orders are orders so let's get this done!"

It dawned on Zach that this whole thing had been
planned. That the two soldiers were there specifically to
kill him. Why that should be would have to remain a
mystery for the moment. Saving his hide would take all
his concentration, and then some.

"You're tough, boy, I'll grant you that," Harve said as
he slowly rose, his blade gleaming in the sunlight. "And
fast too, even with those chains on."

Zach only had eyes for the knife. Coiled on the balls
of his feet, he waited for the thrust.

"Too bad that breed-loving bitch of yours can't see
this," Harve declared. "It would serve her right for taking
up with the likes of you."

It was the wrong thing to say. The red haze before

Zach's eyes became redder, and with a snarl he lunged at Harve's knife arm. But it was a feint. At the last instant he pivoted and slashed his chain at the bigger man's face. He caught Harve across the nose and the eyes, and the screech that tore from Harve's throat had to be heard clear across the compound.

Blood poured, and Harve frantically swiped a sleeve across his eyes to clear them. In doing so he left his stomach unprotected. All Zach had to do was ram his shackles deep into the other's gut to fold Harve like a sheet of paper. Harve's bloody eyes focused, then widened as Zach's shackles connected with the side of Harve's head, bursting Harve's ear like an overripe pear, and down Harve went.

"My turn!"

A sharp stinging sensation down the middle of Zach's back caused him to stumble forward. Shuffling furiously, he turned to find Walt with a knife of his own, and wearing a maniacal expression.

"I'm going to cut you to ribbons, breed! You'll wish you were dead by the time I'm through!"

Zach glanced down. The other knife was on the ground next to Harve, only a few feet away. But shackled as he was, he couldn't possibly reach it before Walt reached him.

Walt waved the knife in small circles and edged forward. "This was supposed to be easy. We were supposed to bleed you and say you started it and that would be that."

Over at the parade ground there were shouts. A few soldiers were moving toward the stockade.

"Any last words, breed, before I do the deed?" Walt asked.

"You talk too much," Zach said, and lunged as if trying for the knife on the ground. Walt was expecting it, and speared his blade at Zach's neck. Almost too late, Zach sidestepped. Grabbing Walt's wrist, he wrenched, and was rewarded with a yelp of pain. But Walt held on to the knife, even when Zach twisted the wrist as hard and as sharp as he could.

Suddenly Walt placed an elbow against Zach's chest, and pushed. Zach tried to stay on his feet but gravity took over and the next thing he knew, he was flat on his back and Walt had a knee on his chest and was raising the knife.

Zach flung his arms up to ward off the descending stroke. Suddenly his forearms were seized. Harve had recovered, and although bleeding from both eyes and his ruin of an ear, he was doing his part to help Walt.

"I've got him! Get it done, damn it!"

Walt's eyes were pools of hate. "Gladly!" He arched his back, then grinned. "This is what you get for bucking your betters."

There was a loud crack and Walt's right shoulder spewed blood and bone and gore. His arms fell and he sagged.

"No!" Harve cried. Wresting the knife from Walt's fingers, he spun and stabbed at Zach's chest. There was another crack and Harve jerked halfway around and keeled to the ground, a bullet hole in his side.

In the doorway to the cell block stood Colonel Templeton, the post commander, with a smoking revolver in his right hand. He strode over, rolled Walt off Zach, and helped Zach to his feet. "Are you hurt?"

"Who sent them to kill me?"

Colonel Templeton turned Zach partway around. "You've got a nasty cut but it missed your spine. I'll send Major Webber over from the infirmary to bandage you up."

"Why did you save me?"

"Why wouldn't I? Count your lucky stars I was near enough to hear the commotion." Troopers were running from all directions and cries had broken out all over. Colonel Templeton took hold of Zach's left arm and hauled him inside. "I only wounded them because I know who sent them."

"What do you mean? These aren't your own men?"

"They came with General Risher. He'll be mad as hell but there's nothing he can do without revealing his hand. I'll get the doctor for them as soon as you're safe."

Confusion jumbled Zach's thoughts. He had met Risher and disliked the man intensely. The general had not disguised the fact that he wanted Zach found guilty, and hanged. "I don't understand. Why would he try to have me killed when in his eyes I'm as good as dead anyway?"

"If he had wanted you dead, you would be dead."

They were at Zach's cell by then and Colonel Templeton ushered him in, closed the door, and wheeled around. "I'll give orders that from now on you're not to be taken from your cell without my express permission."

"Wait! You can't just walk off."

"Yes, I can." Colonel Templeton never looked back, and in a few moments the door at the far end of the cell block clanged shut behind him.

Chapter Six

Stanley P. Dagget liked to eat his supper at a small place in the heart of Wyandot City. It was run by a heavyset Wyandot woman whose friendly smile never failed to cheer him, and whose fondness for her own food showed how good a cook she was.

This particular evening, Stanley took his table by the front window so he could watch the ebb and flow of humanity, and thought about his meeting with Louisa King. She was a most unusual woman, in his estimation, with a wild streak in her as wide as the Mississippi River. How else to explain her preference for living in the remote Rockies? And for a husband who was only a little less wild than the beasts who shared their domain? She was also uncommonly pretty, but Stanley did not allow himself to dwell on that.

He was sipping his first cup of coffee and waiting for his steak and potatoes when he happened to glance out the window and was amazed to behold the last person he ever expected to see strolling the streets of Wyandot City.

Arthur Hunnicut III was tall and broad-shouldered and strikingly handsome. With his reddish-blond hair and square jaw and twinkling blue eyes, he was the perfect portrait of manhood. His suit was the most expensive money could buy, his shoes polished to a sheen. The smile he bestowed on those he passed was dazzling. In his right hand he held a brass-tipped cane with an ivory knob, which he twirled from time to time.

Stanley sat dumfounded as Hunnicut approached the restaurant and sauntered inside and directly over to his table.

"Stanley! How delightful to see you again."

Awkwardly, Stanley accepted the hand thrust at him, and shook it. As always, Hunnicut nearly broke his fingers. "Arthur," he mumbled.

Hunnicut gazed around the room as he pulled out a chair and sat. "Leave it to you to choose a quaint establishment like this. You really must let me take you to St. Louis sometime and treat you to an evening at the Golden Bough. Now, there's a restaurant fit for true gentlemen."

"I would be happy to," Stanley said, knowing full well he would never receive the invitation.

Hunnicut flicked a speck of lint from the tablecoth and placed his cane in front of him. "You must be wondering what on earth I'm doing here."

"To put it mildly," Stanley conceded.

"I take it you've heard we'll soon be jousting in legal combat?" Hunnicut said with a grin.

"The King case. Yes. Judge Hardesty paid me a visit."

"And me, as well, over a week ago." Hunnicut's grin widened. "To think, you pitted against me. You must be flattered the judge thought of you."

"It was quite unexpected," Stanley said.

Hunnicut laughed as if that was hilariously amusing. "Indeed. When he broached it at the club, I was too grateful for words." Leaning forward, he lowered his voice. "Every newspaper from here to the Atlantic will want news on the trial."

"You regard that as a good thing?"

"Don't you?" Hunnicut rejoined. "This case will make us famous, Stanley."

"Defending my client will be difficult enough without all the publicity. I was thinking of asking Judge Hardesty to impose a gag order and bar reporters from the courtroom."

Hunnicut snapped back as if he had been slapped. "Don't be preposterous, Stanley. If you do that, it defeats the whole purpose."

"The only purpose I'm concerned about is doing all in my power for my client."

"There you go again." Hunnicut toyed with the ivory knob on his cane. "You worry me, Stanley. You truly do. I was right in seeking you out to discover for myself exactly where you stand." He paused. "You see, I know you better than the judge and the general. They didn't take me seriously enough when I told them you were scrupulously, nauseatingly honest. They thought—" He stopped and toyed with the knob.

"It sounds as if you had a much longer talk with them than I did," Stanley observed. "Did you know beforehand that they intended to ask me to represent Zach King?"

"Let's just say I was aware you were one of the leading candidates," Hunnicut said. "They ran the list by me and asked my opinion."

"Isn't that rather unorthodox?"

"So is everything else about this case. This halfbreed is the first renegade the United States government has brought to trial and they dearly want to make an example of him."

"Provided he's found guilty."

Arthur Hunnicut scowled. "Tell me something. What is this breed to you that you should give a good damn what happens to him?"

"He's my client."

For a while Hunnicut was silent. Then, "So you intend to fight for him tooth and nail, is that it?"

"I intend to represent him to the best of my ability, yes. Isn't that what we're required to do as attorneys?"

Hunnicut gazed out the window at the passersby, most of them Wyandot Indians. "Your principles are commendable, Stanley. I don't share them, mind you, but I mean that sincerely. Your naiveté, on the other hand, is not nearly as appealing. You see the world in terms of black and white and that's not how it is. There are shades of gray, Stanley, and this case is one of them."

"I'm afraid I don't follow you."

"I know you don't, Stanley, which makes what I am going to do to you all the more regrettable. But I must get this off my chest. Fate has thrown a golden ring in my lap and I intend to run with it."

Stanley rimmed his coffee cup with a finger. "What is it, exactly, you plan to do?"

Hunnicut locked eyes with him. "I intend to win my case, Stanley, at all costs. I intend to beat you, to humiliate you if I have to, to rub your nose in your lack of experience and general incompetence. Face it. We both know you're not the world's best lawyer."

"You came all this way to insult me?"

"No, Stanley. I only want you to know what you're in for. Think what you will of me, you must concede I am always fair in my personal dealings with my peers."

The Wyandot woman came to refill Stanley's cup and

nothing was said until she had returned to the kitchen.

"I hope I haven't upset you," Hunnicut commented. "Don't take it personally. I wouldn't care if God Almighty were defending this renegade, I'd crush him as I'll crush you."

"Do your best. I don't crush easily."

"I just wanted you to know." Rising, Hunnicut stressed, "Nothing, absolutely nothing, will stand in my way." He offered his hand again.

"You're leaving already?" Stanley braced to have his hand crushed but Hunnicut barely squeezed. "I thank you for being so frank with me, Arthur."

"May the best attorney beat the stuffing out of the other." Grinning, Hunnicut touched his cane to his forehead and departed.

The meal came but Stanley ate it without really tasting it. He was too absorbed in the implications of all he had learned. Certain aspects were troubling. Originally, he thought Judge Hardesty had done him a great honor by selecting him, and was grateful. Now he saw it in another light, and he was angry. Extremely angry.

As he bent his steps toward his lodgings, Stanley was filled with new resolve. On a whim he turned left at the next intersection and was pleased to see the window of the *Wyandot Guardian* aglow with lamplight. The owner often worked late setting type for the next edition. Stanley knew him personally, which was why he didn't bother to knock. A tiny bell tinkled as he opened the door.

"Mr. Dagget? It has been a while since you honored me with a visit."

John Littletree was a full-blooded Wyandot Indian, but in every other respect, from his clothes to the style in which he wore his hair, he was a perfect testament to the Wyandot philosophy of adopting white ways.

The Wyandots were an astute people. They learned from the misfortunes and mistakes of others. They had seen a lot of tribes torn from their homes and forced to live on reservations. They knew about the tribes who had dared oppose the whites and been wiped out. So to the Wyandot, adapting became a matter of survival.

Long ago, the Wyandot elders had held a council and decided the wisest thing for their people to do was to take up white ways and dress as whites did and, in so doing, demonstrate to the whites that they need not be made to live on a reservation or be wiped out.

Stanley was amazed by how completely the Wyandots had changed. Only a few short generations ago they had lived as most other woodland Indians; they wore deerskin clothes, lived in simple lodges, and hunted and raised a few crops for their sustenance. Now they lived in frame homes exactly like those whites lived in. They sent their children to a school patterned after white schools and they ran their businesses every bit as efficiently as their white counterparts. They were a marvel, these Wyandots, and Stanley did not mind living among them one bit.

"I'm sorry to bother you, John, but I need a favor."

Littletree wore an apron smudged with ink and was rifling through a drawer for something, but he dropped what he was doing and came right over. "You have but to ask, my friend."

"You keep copies of your back issues around, don't you?"

"In a room in the back," Littletree said, with a jerk of his thumb at a door at the rear. "Why?"

"I'm looking for every article you've ever printed about Zachary King, the man accused of attacking—"

"The trading post." Littletree finished the sentence for him. "Yes, I know all about him. King is on the tongue of all my people. We would not like it to become common knowledge, but we admire him for what he did."

"You admire a murderer?"

"Is that how you see it? Then come." Littletree led Stanley into the back room, which was tidy and spotless. "Here they are."

The newspapers were stacked on a table against the left wall. Littletree had only been publishing the *Guardian* for five years so the stacks were not that high. He thumbed through one, selecting specific editions, and gave them to Stanley. "I have followed the story closely and reprinted everything the bigger newspapers carry. I have also written up a few things on my own."

"Do you think King is innocent?" Stanley asked.

"No, my friend. He is as guilty as guilty can be. But should he be punished? That is the crucial question. And we believe he should not."

"I never thought I would see the day when the Wyandots condoned killing," said Stanley.

"Cold-blooded murder is one thing. But when a man is protecting his loved ones and his home, then it is not murder, but self-defense."

"How can that apply in this case?"

"Read for yourself and find out." Littletree gave him one last newspaper. "You can use the desk over by the press out front."

Predictably, the first account merely relayed the news that the army believed a trading post in the Green River country had been attacked by hostiles and all the traders slain and the post burned to the ground.

The next article, which cited Colonel Templeton at Fort Leavenworth as the source, mentioned that the army planned to send a patrol under Lieutenant Phillip Pickforth to investigate, and that the brother of the man who owned the trading post, one Phineas Borke, was going along.

It was months before the massacre again made the news, and then it did so in a most spectacular fashion. Pickforth had returned with a prisoner. His account of the trials and tribulations the patrol had faced made the front page of newspapers all around the nation. He did not say much about King but what he did say was telling: "It's up to a jury to decide his innocence or guilt, but I have never met anyone with such a reckless disregard for living as the law requires."

In an accompanying piece, the basic facts of the attack were restated: Zachary King, at the head of a Shoshone war party, had slain seven white men, including Artemis Borke, the head of the Ham's Fork Trading Post, and all those who worked for him. In addition, an undetermined number of Crows were killed.

Near the end of the account was a tidbit Stanley found interesting; the attack was the first and only known instance of Shoshone hostility toward whites. Until then, the Shoshones were considered the friendliest tribe in the Rockies.

Stanley took a small pad from a pocket and scribbled notes.

The next news item was notable for containing excerpts of the only recorded interview Zach King gave. It was conducted by a reporter for the *St. Louis Star*. The reporter described King as "truculent and savage," and as having "the beady eyes of an animal." Hardly impartial reporting, Stanley thought.

The reporter repeatedly ridiculed King's claim that the traders were unscrupulous and that King was only helping his friends, the Shoshones. One paragraph read: *It is well and good for this wild man of the mountains to try and justify his vile deeds now that he has been brought to bay and faces imprisonment or worse, but need it be noted that lies comes easily to his kind, and that to save his life he would say anything?*

The last paragraph also caught Stanley's eye: *There must come an end to tolerance and forbearance. Zachary King stands for all that is inimical to the white race and our manifest destiny. We must send a clarion message to others of his ilk by showing them that when it comes to heinous crimes of this nature, we will follow the Biblical injunction of an eye for an eye.*

There were other accounts but they contained nothing new. One piece, written by Littletree, gave Stanley food for thought: *Zachary King has been vilified as a heartless fiend. But is it heartless to stand up for one's people? He has been called an evil savage. But is it evil to oppose evil? In the rush to judgement, the rule of law must not be ignored. Of what value is a law if it is not administered fairly? Of what value is justice if it is not tempered by wisdom and mercy? Zachary King will not be the only one on trial; America itself, and all that this great country stands for, will also be put to the acid test of fairness and truth.*

Stanley leaned back, and for the longest while was deep in thought.

Chapter Seven

Nate King was worried. They had been riding so long and so hard that the wear was showing on their mounts. He couldn't stop fretting that one would go lame, and even though he was half expecting it, he was still angry when it actually happened. It was the middle of the morning and they were riding at a brisk walk, all of them as anxious as ever to reach Fort Leavenworth as soon as possible.

"I must stop!" Blue Water Woman called out, and promptly drew rein.

One glance, and Nate wanted to indulge in a rare string of cuss words. Her horse was favoring its right foreleg. He joined Shakespeare in examining it and they came to the same conclusion.

"My wife will have to ride double with me," Shakespeare said, "but that will slow us down considerably. The rest of you should go on ahead and we'll catch up when we can."

"Just leave you, Uncle?" This from Evelyn, who adored the McNairs and, like her brother, regarded them as the aunt and uncle she had never known.

Smiling, Shakespeare put a hand on the pommel of her saddle. "Don't fret none over us, fair Ophelia. We can fend for ourselves. It's Zach you should worry about. He needs you, missy, you and all your family."

"But you're family too," Evelyn said.

"She's a beagle, true-bred, and one that adores me. What o' that?" Shakespeare quoted. "You flatter me, girl, beyond all measure. And as family, I urge you to ride on and not give a second thought to us."

"We will be fine," Blue Water Woman said.

Nate did not want to leave them, either. McNair was more than a friend and mentor; he was more like a father. Nate loved the old man as dearly as he loved his wife and his children. But with one of those children in dire jeopardy, his choices were limited. "We're going on. When you reach the post, you should find us camped nearby."

Shakespeare nodded. "Then off with you. And whatever you do, Horatio, don't do anything foolish."

"I'm not stupid," Nate said.

"True. But I know you as well as I know myself, and I know you won't let them string Zach up, if it comes to that. You'd as soon die yourself."

Nate clucked to his bay and did not stop again until the sun was in the middle of the sky. His every instinct was to keep riding, but common sense warned him they risked having another of their animals give out on them. So while his wife and daughter rested in the shade and the horses nipped at grass, he walked into the trees and sat on a log to think. He had been doing a lot of that lately. Thinking about his son, about how he had reared him, and whether he had failed in some regard.

A shadow fell across him. Nate said in the Shoshone language without looking up, "I want to be alone."

Touch The Clouds grunted. "So did I, Grizzly Killer, the summer my oldest son was mauled by a silver bear in the geyser country. For many sleeps he was between this world and the next, until the healer's medicine restored him to me."

"I remember."

"It can turn a man's heart bitter when those who mean the most to him are in need. He has thoughts he would not think if his heart were not hurting."

"First my wife, then Carcajou, now you. Did the three of you sit down together last night and decide to take turns?"

The giant squatted and folded his huge arms across his tree-trunk thighs. "We speak because we care. You have been a brother to me. We have shared much, done much. I would not lose you."

"I would not lose my son." Nate looked at him. "I will do what I must to keep him alive. Is that what you want to hear?"

"Let us speak with straight tongues so I know where my brother's heart is." Touch The Clouds paused. "When you say you will do what you must, will you kill these whites who have taken Stalking Coyote?"

"If I have to."

"What then, Grizzly Killer? What will the whites do?"

"They will come after us, and if they cannot catch us, they will call us outcasts. Or as whites say, outlaws. They will put a price on our heads and any white who finds us can kill us."

"What of my cousin, your wife? What of Blue Flower, your daughter?"

Nate pursed his lips. His friend was only trying to be helpful but he resented being treated as if he were not mature enough to make his own decisions. "We will live as we always have."

"Where? In your wooden lodge near Eagle Peak? The whites will find you and kill you. What of your family then?"

"Is there a point to all this?"

"Let me do what must be done. If there is killing to do, I will do it. Stalking Coyote can come live with our people and if the whites try to kill him or take him, it is the whites who will die."

The full import of what the warrior was suggesting took a few moments for Nate to absorb. A warm sensation spread through him and he had to look away. "I cannot ask you to do such a thing."

"Many winters ago, when we were young like your son, my people took you as one of our own. That which I would do for you, I would do for any of them."

Among the Shoshones, Touch The Cloud was a giant in more than stature. His heart, as the Shoshones liked to say, was as big as the sky. He always put the welfare of his people before all else. When a family was without food, he shared some of his. When a warrior did not have a horse, he gave one from his own herd. He cared, truly cared, and his reputation for kindness and generosity was as great if not greater than his reputation as a warrior. This, more than anything else, was why his people looked up to him as the leader of their band, and perhaps, one day, as the leader of the entire tribe.

Nate was touched by the offer. He never expected it, since he still tended to think as whites did and to regard a man's problems as his own. The offer was all the more surprising because Touch The Clouds was fully aware of the consequences. Which, in themselves, were why Nate said, "I am honored, but no."

"Because he is your son?"

"Because it would lead to bad blood between the Shoshones and the whites. Because the whites will think of the Shoshones as they do the Sioux and the Blackfeet and the Apache. As enemies to be destroyed. I could not live with that." Nate gripped the warrior's shoulder. "I thank you, though, my brother."

Nate's spirits were a little lighter when they rode on. But when the sky darkened to the west, so did his mood. A storm was sweeping in from across the plains. Flashes of lightning slashed a gigantic cloud bank, and the keen of distant winds gradually swelled.

"We must seek shelter, husband," Winona said, with a nod at Nature's tantrum.

Were Nate alone, he would brave the elements, and the risk be damned. But now he scoured the woods on either side of the trail until he spied a bluff a short way to the north. "This way!" he shouted, and with a wave of his arm, he left the trail and trotted through a strip of woodland to the bluff's base. It was high enough to shield them from the worst of the wind and some of the rain. Dismounting, he held Evelyn's reins as she swung down.

"Are we safe here, Pa?"

"As safe as anywhere," Nate answered. They had experienced the terrible and ruthless power of such storms before, each one an occurrence they did not care to repeat.

The nearby trees were bending and whipping in invisible hands. The grass rippled, bent by invisible feet. Birds were taking frantic wing eastward in a futile bid to outfly the tempest. A doe came bounding out of a thicket, stood quivering a moment, then bleated and bounded off.

Minutes later the storm unleashed its full fury.

*   *   *

Stanley P. Dagget was supposed to pick Lou up at noon
for the long ride to the post. He wanted to rent a buckboard instead of going horseback, which she let on was
fine with her but which added an unwanted complication
to her plan.

Lou spent the early part of the morning in front of the
full-length mirror on the closet door. She had gone to a
general store down the street and bought a dagger and a
derringer, using up more of the few dollars she had left.
But it was worth it if her scheme worked out.

The problem was how to smuggle the weapons into the
fort. On her previous visits the guards had frisked her.
She always objected but they laughed and insulted her and
frisked her anyway. One soldier had summed up the feelings of them all by saying, "This is what you get for
taking up with a breed. No decent gal would let an animal
like him touch her."

Lou had dearly yearned to bash his face with her fists
but she had settled for biting her lip and swallowing the
indignity. She had to, or they would deny her the privilege
of seeing her husband.

Standing in front of the mirror, Lou recalled each visit.
She remembered where the guards had touched her, and
more to the point, where they hadn't. One spot was between her shoulder blades, another on the inside of her
thighs. And then there were always her moccasins.

Lou experimented. She tried hiding the derringer in her
moccasin but the moccasin bulged suspiciously and the
derringer chafed her skin when she walked.

She cut a rope the right length and tied one end to the
dagger and then looped the other around her neck and

dangled the knife between her shoulder blades but the rope showed when she bent down or moved certain ways.

She cut two shorter lengths and tied the derringer to her right thigh and the knife to her left thigh. Her britches didn't bulge all that much and she could move freely, but to get hold of them she had to drop her pants and that didn't appeal to her.

Lou slumped on the sofa, at a loss. She could bake Zach a pie or a cake with the weapons hidden inside but the guards were bound to inspect any food. They were crude and spiteful but they were efficient at their jobs. Soldiers had to be. Discipline in the military was harsh.

She held the derringer in one hand and the knife in the other, and hefted them. Looking down at herself, she noticed that her buckskin pants fit loosely from her knees to her feet. Bending, she pulled up her left pant leg, pressed the knife against the back of her calf, and tied it in place. When she lowered the pant leg back down and stood, there was no bulge to speak of.

Lou tied the derringer to her other calf, then walked back and forth across the room. So long as she was careful, both weapons would stay in place, and to reach them, all she had to do was slide a hand up her pantlegs.

Gazing at her reflection in the mirror, Lou smiled and said out loud, "Soon, my love. Soon."

At eleven-thirty she washed her face and brushed her hair and double-checked the knots. She was out front waiting when the buckboard arrived.

Stanley P. Dagget wore the same clothes as the day before. He doffed his bowler and started to climb down to help her up, but Lou vaulted into the seat and said excitedly, "Let's go!"

"I must say, your enthusiasm is commendable," Dagget commented as he flicked the reins. "It's nice to see you've shaken off the doldrums."

"I sure have," Lou said, and giggled girlishly at the thought of her secret. Before the day was out Zach would be free and in her arms. "Thanks to you."

"What a nice compliment," Dagget said. "I just hope your husband will be as agreeable. I read in the newspaper that they keep him shackled hand and foot because he has struck several soldiers."

"You can believe what you want but Zach is never violent except when he has to be."

"I have never had to be violent once my whole life, Mrs. King."

"Have you ever had a Sioux warrior out to split your skull? Or been charged by a griz? Or had a pack of winter-starved wolves think you'd make a tasty meal?"

"Your point being, I presume, that I haven't had to be violent because I don't live in a violent environment?"

Lou giggled again. She couldn't help herself. Now that she had committed herself, a great weight had been lifted from her shoulders. "It's a good thing you're a lawyer."

"I beg your pardon?"

"You sure talk like one." Lou clapped him on the shoulder. "But I like you anyway, Stanley P. Dagget." Today, she liked everyone. "And you sure do blush easy."

Dagget's cheeks were pink again. "Forgive my boldness, but you are a most unusual woman. Perhaps the most unusual I have ever met."

"I'm no different than any other."

"On the contrary. You wear pants, for one thing, which

no other woman of my acquaintance has ever done. You cut your hair like a man and talk boldly like a man, and if I did not know you were married, I would think you were more man than woman."

Lou thought that just about the silliest thing she ever heard. "It doesn't do to judge folks by the clothes they wear. It's what's inside the clothes that makes them who they are."

"Another perceptive point. I can't help but wonder if your crude antics aren't a sham. You're much smarter than you give the impression of being."

"Thanks. I think," Lou said, and after that they did not say anything for mile after long, dusty mile. She noticed that when she moved her right leg, the dagger jiggled slightly. Evidently, when she swung onto the seat, the rope had come a little loose. In her excitement she had neglected to be careful, and now she was filled with fear that the dagger would slip free. To keep that from happening before they reached the fort, she pressed her legs tight together.

"Have you decided to take my advice and buy a dress for the trial?" Dagget abruptly inquired.

"If I have to, I will, yes."

"I can't recommend it highly enough." They were climbing a grade. Beside the road on the left was a blackened stump, all that was left of a lightning-blasted tree. At sight of it, the lawyer made a point of sitting straighter and smoothing his jacket. "We're almost there. I trust you're ready to persuade your husband I have his best interests at heart?"

"You and me, both," Lou said.

Chapter Eight

Shakespeare McNair had seen a lot of storms over the course of his many years on the frontier but few rivaled the unfettered might of this one. As soon as he spotted the churning cloud bank to the west he wisely sought a safe haven. But they were in a low-lying area and the only shelter was the undergrowth.

He led Blue Water Woman and their horse toward the middle of a dense thicket, using his knife and a downed tree limb to hack and smash a path.

Blue Water Woman was unconcerned. She had endured as many storms as he had, and she had learned to accept Nature's tantrums as yet another of the harsher aspects of life in the wild. As he began creating a path, she drew her knife to lend a hand.

Shakespeare glanced at her, and chuckled.

"Has something struck your funny bone?" Blue Water Woman, like Winona King, had struggled long and hard to learn the white man's tongue and had mastered it as no other Flathead ever had.

"You look mighty pretty swinging that thing," Shakespeare said, and added from one of his favorite plays, "Oh speak again, bright angel! For thou art as glorious to this night, being over my head, as is a winged messenger of heaven."

"For one thing, it is not night." Blue Water Woman chopped a small limb. "For another, I am not an angel."

"You don't have a shred of romance in your soul, wench."

"Then why have you stayed with me so long?" Blue Water Woman shot back.

"I like how you snore."

Blue Water Woman checked a swing of her knife to say, "You are a cad, sir, and a lunatic besides."

"Excellent. Well done. Another couple of years and you'll be able to hold your own with me."

"Matching wits with a half-wit is no great accomplishment."

"Ouch," Shakespeare said, and now it was he who paused. "Have you been reading my complete works of William S. behind my back?"

"Only late at night when *your* snoring keeps *me* awake."

"Zounds. I've been outmaneuvered. You are a credit to your gender, fair Katrina."

"Are you implying I am a shrew?"

Shakespeare chortled and renewed his advance into the thicket, his razor-edged knife and makeshift club creating a wide swath. He didn't stop until they reached the heart of the tangle, and once there, he cleared enough space for their horse and themselves.

Blue Water Woman was at his side every step and swing of the way, and when the work was done, they stood panting and grinning at each other.

"We're getting too old for this, my dear," Shakespeare said. "And Nate wonders why I don't gallivant around as much as I used to? The boy has no conception of what it's like to get up in the morning and have all your joints so stiff and your muscles so sore, you can barely move."

"You were quite spry the night before we left," Blue Woman Woman commented. "Or was that a younger man in my bed?"

"Hussy," Shakespeare said.

"Satyr."

Shakespeare threw back his head and roared. "That was marvelous. I swear, there are times when I'm so damn proud to be your bedmate, I could bust for joy."

Blue Water Woman pretended to pout. "Is that all I am, then? A warm body on a cold night? Soft lips on that gristle you call a beard?"

"Ouch again." Shakespeare would have said more but at that instant a tremendous blast of wind shook the thicket and a vivid bolt of lightning sheared the rapidly darkening sky. Thunder boomed, and they crouched face to face, Shakespeare holding fast to the reins of their frightened mount. "Have I told you lately I love you?"

"As husbands go, you are one of the best," Blue Water Woman said tenderly.

"Had a lot of them, have you?" Shakespeare grinned and pecked her on the tip of her nose.

That was the last either of them could say for a while. Shrieking winds tore at their sanctuary as outside their haven, tree limbs were snapped like twigs and the trees were bent in half. Thunderbolt after thunderbolt cleaved the ink-black clouds, the din a continuous cannonade that assaulted the eardrums and shook the very air.

Shakespeare put his free arm around his wife and held her close. Although he was soon soaked to the skin and his beaver hat was whipped into the ethereal realm and lost forever and the horse kept prancing and trying to bolt, he was as happy as happy could be because he was with the woman he adored.

Shakespeare had often heard it said that after a while marriage lost its luster. Many a man had told him as much, many a friend had complained of a marriage that went from exciting and fun to dull and boring. But not his. Every day he discovered his love for her anew. Maybe it was because they married so late in life after fate had cruelly torn them apart years ago, but every morning, without fail, he gave thanks for their time together, for every precious minute, every precious second.

Nate once asked if he resented being separated from Blue Water Woman all those years, and to that Shakespeare had responded that yes, of course, it made him mad as hell. But he wouldn't harp on it. He wouldn't let it fester inside and sour him on life. Bad things happened. Bad things happened to good people. As another book besides the Bard's had it, time and chance happened to all men, and there was nothing anyone could do about it.

A crackling bolt from out of the maelstrom struck a tree a stone's throw from the thicket and the air around them sizzled like frying bacon. Shakespeare felt his skin tingle, and gripped the reins tighter to keep their horse from running off.

In recent months he had been thinking more of that other book. No one lived forever, as much as they would like to, and it was as plain as the white hairs on his head and chin that he was getting on in years and had few left to live. Maybe five years, if he was lucky. Ten if the Good Lord was feeling charitable.

The flash of another bolt illuminated the thicket, and Blue Water Woman. She was looking at him. Their eyes

met, and Shakespeare kissed her on the mouth, then
smiled. Despite the cyclonic winds and the sheets of pelting rain and the thunderous din, he had rarely felt so serene inside, so at peace with the world and with himself.

Then an acrid scent filled his nose, and Shakespeare
twisted and discovered the thicket was on fire.

Miles to the east, Nate King did not feel at all serene. He
was furious at the storm, furious at the delay it had caused,
furious at life in general for the injustice inflicted on his
son. The savage tempo of the storm matched the whirlwind of anger deep in his heart.

Nate had always tried to live a good, decent life. He
always strived to do his best by his family and friends.
He had done his share of things he was not proud of, but
overall, he could hold his head high. Which made the dire
straits his son was in all the more unfair.

Zach had only been trying to do what was best. Nate
himself had impressed on the boy from an early age that
a man should always do the right thing. His own father,
as stern an individual as ever lived, has impressed it on
him, often with the aid of a switch or a belt. From father
to son to son—and look at what had come of it.

Nate knew he shouldn't blame himself. Zach had always been a hothead and much too often let his temper
get the better of him. But this wasn't one of those times.
Zach had only done what was necessary to protect the
Shoshones. And since when was it wrong to stand up for
one's people?

The crash of thunder ended Nate's reverie. Above them
indigo clouds roiled, disgorging torrents of rain and an
unending barrage of lightning and thunder.

Winona and Evelyn were huddled by the bluff, Evelyn hugging her mother.

Touch The Clouds stood tall and impassive, his arms folded, oblivious to the rain pelting him in sheets.

Holding firmly to the bay's reins, Nate sidled close to his wife and daughter. "How are you holding up, little one?" he shouted above the cacophony of sound.

"I'm wet as wet can be," Evelyn replied.

"We'll dry you out in no time once this ends," Nate yelled.

Another bolt struck close to the bluff and Evelyn jumped. "I don't like all this lightning."

Neither did Nate. He knew of two frontiersmen and several Indians who had been killed by it when they were caught out in the open in a thunderstorm. Old Jonas Wainright had been on his mule when he was hit, and Jonas and the mule had been charred to a cinder.

"I hope it ends soon," Evelyn hollered.

"We could be here for hours," Winona shouted.

Nate hoped not. They would lose the rest of the day. But she might be right. The storm stretched from horizon to horizon and there was no sign of a break or a letup.

Suddenly Evelyn gave another start, and pointed. "Pa! Look there!"

Shifting, Nate stared into the woods but he didn't see anything until another brilliant bolt from on high lit up the landscape.

The storm was wreaking havoc with the wildlife. Already they had seen deer and several raccoons in flight, and once a red fox that raced by the bluff with its head low and paid no more attention to them than if they were rocks or grass. Now the storm had driven a black bear into the open, one of the largest black bears Nate had ever beheld. It was only a dozen yards away, facing into the storm with its teeth bared as if it would attack the elements themselves.

At that instant Evelyn's horse nickered. It didn't like the thunder and had been growing increasingly skittish.

Nate was about to reach for its reins when he saw the bear turn and stare at them. Its muzzle lifted and it sniffed the wind. Ordinarily, black bears ran off at the sight of a human being. But there were exceptions, as there were to everything in life. When they were incited enough or hungry enough, black bears were as fierce and deadly as grizzlies.

This one moved slowly toward them, still sniffing. Bears relied on their sense of smell more than any other sense, but the storm was dampening the scent. The black bear knew something was there at the base of the bluff but it didn't know what.

Nate had his rifle in his left hand. But in order to shoot he had to let go of the bay's reins, which he was loathe to do. The bay might run off, delaying them further. Raising his face into the wind and the rain, he hollered, "Make yourself scarce, you stupid bear!"

The shout brought the black bear to a halt but it didn't run off. It was staring at Touch The Cloud's paint as if it were entertaining the notion of feasting on fresh horse flesh.

Black bears ate just about anything. Fish and berries were high on their diet. So were roots and grubs. But they would eat whatever they could catch, whether it be a squirrel, a fawn, or something a lot larger, like a man or a horse.

Nate used to think of black bears as nuisances. Grizzlies were the ones he always looked out for. Compared to thousand-plus pound grizzlies with their four- to five-inch claws and teeth nearly as long, a typical black bear, which seldom weighed more than five hundred pounds, was rather puny.

From firsthand experience, Nate knew how ferocious grizzlies could be. His Indian name, Grizzly Killer, was more fitting than he had ever wanted it to be. When he initially came west, the plains and mountains were over-run by the huge bears. Every time he turned around he was bumping into one. Or so it seemed. And because he had no hankering to end his days in a griz's belly, he had killed them. Killed a lot of them.

His reputation as a bear-killer spread far and wide. Shakespeare McNair was of the opinion that Nate had slain more grizzlies than any man alive. Which was ironic, given that Shakespeare and a few others had lived in the mountains a lot longer than he had. But as McNair once put it, "I don't know what it is about you, Horatio, but you draw silver-tips like flowers draw bees. If there's a griz within a hundred miles, it will go out of its way to turn you into grizzly shit."

McNair exaggerated, as always, but not by much.

Given his experience with grizzlies, it was no wonder Nate had regarded black bears as minor pests until not long ago when one had nearly killed him. A young black bear, no less, not a fourth the size of some of the grizzlies he had encountered.

Now here was another black bear, a much larger one, plodding toward them with the methodical gait of a pred-ator stalking prey.

"I'm scared, Pa!" Evelyn yelled.

"I won't let it hurt you," Nate shouted.

Winona was trying to tuck the stock of her rifle to her shoulder but her horse had spotted the approaching carnivore and was acting up.

Nate wrapped the bay's reins around his wrist and snapped his Hawken up to fire. He wouldn't let it come another step.

Just then the black bear stopped.

Nate waited, not wanting to shoot it if he didn't have to. His first shot might not kill it, and wounding a bear invariably provoked it to attack.

Touch The Clouds had unslung his bow and nocked an arrow to the string. But, like Nate, he was waiting to see what the bear would do.

To Nate's relief the black bear started to turn away. Nate figured it had caught their scent at last and wanted no part of them. He lowered his Hawken, but not all the way, not until he was sure they were safe.

That was when a new sound reached Nate's ears. A sound he couldn't quite identify. Since it was faint he leaped to the conclusion that it must be coming from a long way off. But then he realized the sound was much closer than he thought but was being smothered by the deluge. He cocked his head, trying to pinpoint where it came from.

"Husband!" Winona cried. She had turned. One arm was upraised, and she was pointing.

Nate looked over his shoulder. He thought for a second he must be seeing things, that it was a trick of the rain and the dark and the wind. But it was no trick, and an icy chill gripped him clear down to his marrow.

The side of the bluff was breaking away. Loosened by the downpour, tons of earth and rock were peeling loose, like the peel of an apple being pared away by a knife. An enormous slide had started.

A slide that was coming down right on top of them.

Chapter Nine

Fort Leavenworth was situated on high bluffs on the west bank of the Missouri River and when Louisa King had first set eyes on it, it was nothing like she expected it to be. For one thing, it lacked the log ramparts of other frontier forts she had seen. Instead, it was laid out more like a town. There was a headquarters building, officers' quarters, barracks for the companies of troops, stables for the cavalry mounts, and quaint white-washed cottages for married personnel, all arranged on three sides of a square that opened onto the prairie.

The stockade sat off by itself, as if shunned. It was a low, squat building, as ugly as a building could be, in Lou's opinion. She couldn't look at it without having to suppress a shudder.

Lou expected to go there as soon as she and Dagget arrived, but a soldier informed the lawyer that the base commander wanted to see them, and directed them to the commander's house. It was the most substantial on the post, made of brick instead of logs, with a neatly trimmed lawn.

Dagget brought the buckboard to a stop and hopped

down. "Permit me, Mrs. King," he said, coming around and reaching up to help her.

Lou let him. She carefully unfurled her legs and took a few short, slow steps to test whether the dagger would slip. She dearly wanted to retie the rope but that was out of the question.

The lawyer misconstrued. "Don't be nervous, Mrs. King. I'll be at your side the whole time."

In answer to his knock, the door was opened by Colonel Templeton, whom Lou had talked to twice before. "Welcome, the both of you. Mrs. King, how nice to see you again. And you're Mr. Dagget, I take it?"

"This is most courteous of you to invite us to your home," Stanley P. Dagget said. "I would have thought you would be waiting for us at your office or the stockade."

"You'll understand why shortly," the officer said. "Suffice it to say I wanted to speak to you in private."

Templeton ushered them into a study and bid them take chairs in front of an oak desk. "I would offer you refreshments but I sent my wife and my orderly away so we could be alone."

Lou noticed that Dagget had grown somber. It struck her that this must be serious, indeed, for the colonel to have gone to such lengths, and she blurted out her foremost fear: "Has something happened to my husband?"

"I'm afraid he was attacked by two troopers, but he wasn't seriously hurt."

Forgetting herself and the need to move slowly, Lou sprang to her feet, then promptly sat back down again. "Attacked? How can anyone get at him when he's locked in a cell?"

"It was during his exercise period." Colonel Templeton

slumped into his chair. He appeared tired, almost haggard, and when he looked at Lou his eyes were deeply troubled. "Had I not happened along, your husband would be in the infirmary."

"We appreciate you taking the time to personally inform us," Dagget said.

"There's more," Colonel Templeton responded, but instead of elaborating, he wearily rubbed his face, then sighed. "Twenty years ago I would not have done what I did, knowing what I do."

Lou was confused and she wasn't the only one.

"You're speaking in riddles, sir," Dagget remarked.

"Not really. You see, I retire next year, so it's not as if my career is at stake. Others aren't so fortunate. They must do as they're ordered whether they agree with those orders or not."

"I still don't follow you, Colonel."

"The fight in the exercise yard wasn't a random occurrence, Mr. Dagget. Need I say more, or can you see where this is leading?"

If the lawyer couldn't, Lou sure could. "Someone is out to murder my husband, is that it? Is there another Borke running around I don't know about?"

Colonel Templeton turned toward a window and the glare of the sunlight added ten years to his features. "The Borke brothers have a sister, I understand, but she won't be at the trial. But no, she wasn't involved. This stream, Mrs. King, has a much higher source."

Dagget's eyebrows nearly met over his nose. "Can you speak plainly, Colonel? I, for one, am quite confused."

"I've already said more than I should. I wouldn't have said this much except that I refuse to dishonor the uniform

I wear by condoning the actions of my superiors. My oath of allegiance is to my country, not to them." Templeton stared at Lou. "But there is one thing I can make clear. The attack wasn't an attempt on your husband's life, Mrs. King. Murdering him wouldn't serve their purpose."

"Then why attack him at all?" Lou asked.

"To show him for the vicious savage they've made him out to be." The colonel gazed across the post. "They would have cut him, and cut him badly, then leaked word to the newspapers."

"What good would that do them?"

"They would cast the blame on his shoulders, saying he instigated it, further prejudicing the public against him. It's in their best interests to tarnish Zach to where everyone believes he's guilty before he ever sets foot in a courtroom."

"Trial by the press?" Dagget said. "That's dastardly devious."

"And effective, too, if they can get away with it. The two soldiers responsible are in the infirmary and have refused to talk. I want to convene a court martial but my superiors will contrive an excuse not to, and the pair will be transferred and mysteriously disappear. That's how these things work."

All this was so new and bewildering, Lou couldn't quite grasp it. She knew the army wanted Zach punished but she never imagined they would go to such lengths to bolster their case against him.

"Your husband, Mrs. King, is to be an object lesson for hostiles and renegades everywhere. By hanging him, our government hopes to prevent future incidents like the trading post massacre." Templeton was still gazing out the window. Suddenly he stood and faced them. "That's all I have to say at this time. Report to the stockade. Sergeant Rotowski is under strict orders to admit you and comply with any requests you have."

What Lou had were a dozen burning questions, but Dagget saw her open her mouth and put a finger to his lips. Then he crooked his fingers to indicate she should follow him. "We thank you, Colonel, for your time and consideration."

"Don't make more out of it than there is, Mr. Dagget. I'm only doing what I must to soothe my conscience. You'll forgive me if I don't see you to the door."

The moment they let themselves out, Lou whirled on the lawyer. "Why didn't you want me to say anything? I should have given him a piece of my mind—"

"No, you shouldn't," Dagget interrupted. "He's the one friend we have. Antagonizing him would serve no purpose." He glanced beyond her, and stiffened.

Striding toward the house were two officers: General Risher and Lieutenant Pickforth. Lou disliked both of them. The general treated her with unconcealed contempt, and Pickforth had designs on her unsuitable for a married woman.

"General Risher!" Dagget declared. "What a pleasure to see you and the lieutenant again."

"What are you doing here?" Risher brusquely demanded.

"We're here to see Mrs. King's husband."

"No, I meant, what are you doing *here*." General Risher nodded at the house. "If you need to talk to the colonel you should visit him at headquarters, not at his private residence."

"It was his—" Lou began, but the lawyer stepped in front of her.

"My apologies, General. I'm understandably eager to begin work and wanted to be certain I've been granted unlimited access to my client."

"I should think that would go without saying," General Risher said, some of his suspicion fading.

"Now if you'll excuse us," Dagget said. Taking Lou by the elbow, he smiled and hurried toward the buckboard. In her ear he whispered, "We must be careful what we say around that man."

Lou permitted him to boost her onto the seat. She saw Pickforth grin at her and wished she had her rifle so she could shoot him dead. Holding her chin high, she avoided looking at him.

Dagget parked the buckboard beside the stockade and helped her down. She had taken about six steps when she felt the dagger begin to slide from under the rope. Instantly, she came to a stop.

"Is something the matter?" Dagget asked.

"I feel a little queasy," Lou lied. "It's the thought of those soldiers attacking my husband."

"That's perfectly natural," Dagget sympathized. "Would you care to sit down?" He indicated a bench against the wall.

"No. I want to see Zach." Lou moved slowly so the dagger wouldn't slip any further.

Sergeant Rotowski was waiting for them and escorted them down the hall. Lou didn't like him, either, or how his beady eyes roved hungrily over her buckskins.

They were almost to Zach's cell when it hit her she hadn't been frisked. All the trouble she had gone to in order to smuggle the weapons in, and she could just as easily have concealed them under her shirt.

As always, Lou's heart leaped when she saw the familiar hunkered form of the man she loved. As always, the sight of him so dirty and bedraggled and depressed tore at her like a saber. She forgot herself and ran the last few yards to cling to the bars and exclaim, "It's me, Zach!"

Zach rose and came to the door but had to step back again at a command from Sergeant Rotowski, who took his sweet time opening it, and who locked it again behind them.

"Give a yell when you're ready to leave. I'll be up front."

Lou threw herself into Zach's arms and held him close, fighting back tears of mixed happiness and sorrow. "Oh, Zach," she whispered. "My sweet, sweet Zach."

Stanley P. Dagget waited to be introduced, then shook Zach's hand with enthusiasm. "I hope you'll believe me when I say I'll do all in my power to have you found innocent and set free."

"Do you work magic, then, lawyer?"

"I give my all to every case. No client can ask for more."

"How do I know I can trust you?" Zach demanded.

Her husband's retort was uncalled for, and Lou said so.

"Can you blame me?" Zach responded. "I wouldn't put it past General Risher to rig the trial from start to finish." He stared at Dagget. "For all I know, this lawyer is really out to bury me."

"You're grossly mistaken," Dagget said. "But if that's how you feel, you're more than welcome to dismiss me and find another attorney to represent you. I warn you, though. You won't find another as committed as I am."

"Words," Zach said. "I am so tired of words."

Pulling him toward a corner, Lou said over her shoulder to the lawyer, "Give us a minute, Stanley."

"Of course."

To Zach, Lou whispered, "You're being unfair. I think he is sincere." She pecked his dirty cheek. "Not that we need him. I've brought a derringer and a dagger along to break you out."

Zach gripped her arms. "Where are they?"

"Tied to my calves."

Zach glanced down, then over at Dagget, who had politely turned his back so they could have some privacy. "Give them to me."

"Right this second?" Lou asked. The cells on either side were occupied, the soldiers in them staring. "Someone is bound to notice."

"I won't stay here another day. They're out to get me, Lou, and I'll be damned if I'll make it easy for them."

Lou tenderly held his head in her hands. "We'll get you out. I promise. But we have to do it smart." She looked at Dagget, then whispered, "Play along with what I do. And trust me."

"There is no one I trust more," Zach said.

Lou rewarded him for that with a kiss on the lips, then moved from the corner. "He's sorry for doubting you, Mr. Dagget. It won't happen again."

The lawyer smiled. "That's quite all right. I would feel the same, were I in his shoes. Or moccasins, as the case might be." He paused. "Now then, suppose we begin."

"In here?" Lou said. "We don't have anything to sit on. And it's so gloomy and dusty."

Dagget considered their surroundings. "A valid point. This is hardly a fitting place to conduct an interview, especially since we might be at it for hours."

"Hours?" Zach repeated.

"Yes, Mr. King. We must go over everything in minute detail. The trading post. Your relationship with the Shoshones. What happened when Lieutenant Pickforth arrived in the Rockies. Everything." Dagget stepped to the bars. "Sergeant Rotowski! If you please!"

The noncom came lumbering down the hall. "What can I do for you, Mr. Dagget?"

"I want a room where we can talk in private."

"That's asking a little much. I was told not to let the breed out of his cell again for any reason without specific orders."

"Then I suggest you go talk to Colonel Templeton. He promised I would have your complete cooperation."

Rotowski scratched his chin. "You could have my office, I suppose. It's small and you would be cramped, but—"

"No buts, Sergeant. You will procure a decent room with chairs and a desk. You will also provide a pitcher of water and glasses and whatever else I require. Is that clear?"

Lou was impressed by Dagget's show of authority and confidence. He didn't know it, but he was playing right into her hands. Grinning at Zach, she whispered, "Soon, my love. Very soon."

Chapter Ten

Shakespeare McNair couldn't see how the thicket was on fire with the rain as heavy as it was. He figured the bolt of lightning that struck the nearby tree was to blame, since he now saw that the tree itself was on fire.

Blue Water Woman had seen the flames, too, and like him she was watching to see if the downpour put them out.

Suddenly there was the sound of sizzling bacon again. Only this time it was louder, much louder, so loud it drowned out the rain and the thunder and the wind. At the same instant there was a flash of light so bright, it hurt Shakespeare's eyes, and a blast that sounded like a cannon going off. He felt his body leave the ground and was dimly aware of tumbling end over end, and then he was not aware of anything until the spatter of light rain on his eyelids flung him back into the world of the living.

Shakespeare lay still, trying to prod his dazed mind into working as it should. He was flat on his back. That much he knew. He felt oddly numb and tried to move his hands and feet. For a few harrowing moments he thought he was paralyzed, but then his arms and his legs responded and he exhaled in relief. Raising his head, he looked down at himself. As near as he could tell he was in one piece. But much to his astonishment, wisps of smoke rose from his buckskins. His astonishment grew when he saw that he had to be twenty yards from the thicket, lying in the open near some trees.

The worst of the storm had passed and the clouds overhead were gray instead of black. The wind had dwindled to a stiff breeze and the boom of thunder was now well to the east.

Shakespeare thought of Blue Water Woman and came up off the ground much faster than he should have. Dizziness racked him. He swayed as he stumbled toward the thicket and hollered her name.

There was no answer. His fear climbing, Shakespeare steadied himself and plowed into what was left of the thicket. Much of it had been flattened and lay like wheat fallen by a scythe. The bushes and the ground were also giving off smoke. He came to the middle and drew back a step in horror.

The bolt had struck their horse. The animal lay on its side, charred black in spots, its tongue distended, its eyes rolled back into its head.

"Blue Water Woman?" Shakespeare took another step, and saw her. She lay on her stomach ten feet from where she had been when the lightning hit. "*Blue Water Woman!*"

Skirting the horse, Shakespeare rushed to her side and knelt. Slowly, fearfully, he eased her onto her back. She bore no marks or wounds. Bending, he pressed an ear to her bosom but he couldn't tell if she was breathing. He snatched her wrist and felt for a pulse, his heart nearly stopping when he thought she didn't have one. But there it was, faint but unmistakable.

"Blue Water Woman?" Shakespeare cradled her head in his lap and brushed clinging strands of wet hair from her face. A tiny moan escaped her. "Heart of my heart?" he said more insistently, and gently wagged her chin. It evoked no response. He thought maybe the light rain falling on her face would revive her as it had revived him, but she didn't stir.

Shakespeare worried that she had been hurt internally. He gently lifted her and carefully carried her under a large oak. The ground there wasn't quite as wet as everywhere else, thanks to the thick branches above. Depositing her next to the trunk, he hurried to find firewood.

He might as well be looking for gold nuggets. The vegetation was soaked. The trees, the brush, the weeds, the grass, everything. Finding something dry seemed impossible. Then he saw a middling-sized log. Quickly, he rolled it over, and as he hoped, underneath the log was dry. Unlimbering his big knife, he chopped and hacked, splitting and splintering the wood. When he had a big enough pile, he hastened to the oak.

His possibles bag was drenched but not the tin box inside in which he kept his fire steel and flint and a small amount of kindling taken from a bird's nest. It was a precaution mountaineers routinely took so they could always start a fire when they needed to.

Shakespeare placed some kindling in the pile of wood and struck the fire steel against the quartz until one of the sparks ignited the kindling and gray tendrils curled into the air. Bending, he puffed on the kindling until the tendrils became small flames. Soon the small flames were large flames, and he smiled in satisfaction.

Blue Water Woman still had not come around. Shakespeare felt her pulse again and was elated to find it stronger. He placed her head on his thigh and caressed her wet hair and shuddered at the thought of how close he had come to losing her. He didn't realize her eyes had opened.

"Why so glum, ornery one? Did you think I would put you to the trouble of finding a new wife?"

Too overcome to respond, Shakespeare smothered her face with kisses and then sat back. "Does that answer your question?" he huskily asked.

"I should be struck by lightning every day if that is how you will behave."

"It was the horse that was struck," Shakespeare enlightened her. "We just happened to be too close. My head is thicker than yours so the jolt didn't do as much damage." The joke reminded him. "How do you feel? I couldn't find anything broken."

"I feel a little numb but otherwise I think I am fine."

"The numbness will pass. Mine did after a while." Shakespeare took her hand in his and squeezed. "Damn, you gave me a scare."

"The horse is dead, I take it?"

Shakespeare nodded. "A fine animal, too. We've had that sorrel going on ten years now. I'll check the packs and whatnot in the morning."

"Do it now so we can dry out whatever can be saved."

"I don't want to leave you alone. What if you need me?"

"How far are we from the thicket?"

Shakespeare looked up. The rain had about stopped and the wind about died. The afternoon sun was sending sparkling shafts of sunlight through the remaining clouds. "I'd say about fifty feet."

"Then I think you can hear me if I cry for help." Blue

Water Woman grinned and pinched his cheek. "You are such a silly dear sometimes."

"One of us has to have a romantic bone or two," Shakespeare grumbled, but he did as she wanted. He always did. He loved her so much, he would do anything, anytime, anywhere.

Smoke no longer rose from the horse. Soon the flies would find it and after that it would be the buzzards and the coyotes and whatever else the stench attracted. His saddle was intact but had char marks and the blanket underneath was singed. He carried everything over to the oak, then went back.

He had to look a long time for their rifles. His lay at the edge of the thicket. Brushing it off, he examined it and whooped for joy. Her rifle was not only covered by brush, it was partly buried, and when he pulled it out, he found the stock had been blasted to smithereens and the barrel was bent. It made him realize even more fully how close he had come to losing her.

One of her pistols was missing, so Shakespeare searched in ever-widening circles until he stumbled on it a good forty feet from where they had been huddled when the lightning struck. It was undamaged.

From one of their parfleches Shakespeare took a bundled section of deer hide and unwrapped the pemmican inside. It was made from buffalo meat that had been jerked, ground fine, and mixed with fat and chokecherries. He gave a piece to her and munched on one himself, savoring the taste. "If there's anything else you want, just ask."

"Have I ever mentioned how sweet you can be whenever I am nearly killed?"

"Ingrate," Shakespeare said, and quoted, "I would rather trust a Fleming with my butter, a Parson Hugh the Welshman with my cheese, an Irishman with my aquavitae bottle, or a thief to walk my ambling gelding, than my wife with herself."

Blue Water Woman grinned. "My, aren't we in a funk."

"I figure it's justified. We'll never catch up to the Kings and Touch The Clouds now, and I want to be there for the trial. If nothing else, I'll gladly testify to Zach's sterling character."

"Sterling, yes, but with a few chips and cracks. The boy has always had too much of a temper."

"Maybe so," Shakespeare conceded, "but he's still as dear to me as if he were our own, and what he did was justified, whether the government agrees or not. A pox on all politicians! They're nothing but simpletons who act like the Almighty gave them the right to lord it over everyone else."

"You have said many times that many of your leaders have been fine men."

"Two or three," Shakespeare begrudged her. "But the current crop can't hold a lick to the likes of George Washington and Thomas Jefferson. What has Zachary Taylor ever done except strut around in his uniform and take credit for battles won by the sweat and the blood of the soldiers under him?"

Blue Water Woman selected another piece of pemmican. "If it upsets you so much, why talk about it?"

"Because it's going to get worse and never get better."

"What is?"

"The meddling. Until now, those of us in the Rockies have been left to do as we please. We've been answerable to no one except ourselves. Zach's arrest is the first sign of the change that's coming. Before we know it, there will be towns and cities everywhere, with more laws than you can shake a stick at."

"What is that white saying I want?" Blue Water Woman put a finger to her chin. "Ah. Yes. Now I remember." She grinned. "Making a mountain from a mole hill."

"Shows how much you know. Remember that newspaper the emigrant bound for the Oregon Country gave us? The government is pushing for folks to head west. They call it Manifest Destiny. One coon wrote that one day America will rule the entire North American continent."

"Do you truly believe it will come to that?"

"We're a restless race. We always think the grass is greener over the next hill, so we're always on the move. There was a time when the Appalachian Mountains were our western boundary but we had to see what was over them, and we ended up pushing all the way to the Mississippi River. Along the way we pushed out all the Indians and drove them like cattle to where they didn't want to be or else wiped them out to the last man, woman and child."

"And you fear the same thing will happen when your people push past the Mississippi?"

Shakespeare had grown grim. "As surely as you're lying there, there will come a day when the Flatheads and the Shoshones and the Sioux and the Blackfeet find themselves in the same situation as the Creeks and the Delawares and the Mohawks once did." He reverted to the Bard. "Shame and eternal shame, nothing but shame."

"My people will never let themselves be rubbed out," Blue Water Woman declared.

"A lot of other tribes said the same thing and now there aren't any of them left to say it anymore." Shakespeare frowned. "I've seen a lot of changes in my long life and I can't say that all of them have been for the better."

"Why worry ahead of time? There is another expression your people use." Blue Water Woman moved a little closer to the fire. "We will cross that bridge when we come to it."

"Then be it so," Shakespeare quoted, and rummaged in a different parfleche for their coffeepot and a pan. "Here I am jabbering when I should be warming your innards with coffee and soup. I am sorry, madam."

"Do you hear me complaining?" Blue Water Woman held her hands near to the flames. "A woman could have no better husband."

"Methinks in thee some blessed spirit doth speak," Shakespeare quoted with a smirk. "And who am I to argue?"

Blue Water Woman grinned. "Life with you is never dull. I never know what will come out of your mouth next."

"You and me, both."

They laughed, and Shakespeare busied himself filling the coffeepot and pan with water from the Platte and placing them on to boil. Drawing his knife, he cut up half a dozen pieces of pemmican and dropped them in the pan, then added a cupful of their meager flour.

"I can do that," Blue Water Woman offered when he was adding coffee grounds to the coffeepot.

"Don't you dare. You're not to move a muscle until we

have you fed and dry." Shakespeare peered to the west. "Another couple of hours and night will fall. We might as well stay put and move on at first light."

"On foot?" Blue Water Woman asked.

"Unless you can sprout wings and fly."

"Be serious."

"Oh. I get it. You want me to tote you piggyback the rest of the way. Shouldn't take us more than a year."

"I would much rather ride."

Shakespeare arched an eyebrow at her. "Who wouldn't? Or maybe you expect me to catch and tame a buffalo by breakfast tomorrow so your ladyship can spare her dainty toes the torture?"

"When was the last time you saw anyone ride a buffalo?"

"Not ever, but I always had a secret hankering to try."

"Only you." Blue Water Woman bit off more pemmican. "If we must ride, and we must if we are to overtake Nate and Winona, we need horses."

Snickering, Shakespeare snapped his fingers, then made a show of looking all around as if he were disappointed. "Damn. I thought for sure one would pop out of thin air."

"Have you forgotten, then?" Blue Water Woman asked.

"Forgotten what?" Shakespeare saw that she was gazing back along the trail. A twinkle came into his eyes, and he said, "You would let me?"

"I would help you."

"You're a bloodthirsty cuss, do you know that?"

Blue Water Woman flashed him her most ravishing smile. "I take after my husband."

Chapter Eleven

The deluge had battered the bluff so violently it was breaking apart. In less than an hour the heavy rain had accomplished what would have taken ages by the process of slow erosion.

Nate King took one look and was galvanized into motion. They only had moments in which to act. "Ride!" he bawled. Grabbing Evelyn, he practically threw his daughter onto her horse and smacked it on the rump. It lit out of there as if he had stabbed it. He whirled to help his wife up but her horse was already flying to the south with her half on and half off, clinging to the mane and the saddle.

Touch The Clouds was on his paint and flying after them.

Nate leaped to his bay, glancing over his shoulder as he did. The slide was gaining momentum and pouring groundward like a river of mud. He swung up and slapped his legs against the horse. In the dark and the rain he had lost sight of the others but he was sure they had made it to safety.

For a few moments Nate thought he would, too. In the excitement of the crisis, however, he had forgotten about the black bear, which didn't realize the danger it was in and stood exactly where he had last seen it. By sheer accident he had spurred the bay in its direction, and now the horse did what any horse would do; it came to a sudden stop, whinnied in fear, and reared.

Nate was caught off guard. He had been concentrating on the breaking bluff, and on the mud slide that would engulf him if he didn't get away quickly enough. His feet weren't in the stirrups, and when the bay reared, it was all he could do to stay in the saddle. The bear growled and swung a huge forepaw at the bay, but missed. Wheeling north, the bay gave a long bound, and Nate, unprepared, was unhorsed. He grabbed for the bay's mane but it was so slick with rain, he couldn't retain his hold.

Nate hit the ground on his back. It wasn't a hard fall and he scrambled to his feet, thinking of the bear and the bear's teeth and claws and what the bear would do to him if he didn't get out of there. He took a couple of steps toward the woods, but then there was a new sound. A sound the thunder and the rain and the wind couldn't drown out. A sound that made Nate think of the squish a foot made when it was pulled out of mud, only this squish was louder and sustained and the mud making it wasn't underfoot, it was oozing toward him like a thing alive.

Nate took a couple more strides, but that was all. For then a giant hand closed around his lower legs and pushed them out from under him. Instinctively, he threw his arms over his head, holding the Hawken aloft as the pressure rose from his knees to his hips. The squishing was loud in his ears.

He was mired in mud to the waist. Mud that was on the move and sweeping him along with it. He tried to free himself but the mud clung fast. He traveled ten feet, then twenty, all the while in dread of the mud rising up over his face and suffocating him.

Gradually the flow stopped. Nate tried to wrench loose but instead sank deeper, up to his chest. He stopped struggling.

Meanwhile, the storm raged unabated. The rain fell in torrents, the wind lashed the land, lightning seared earth and sky. An especially close thunderbolt briefly turned artificial night into artificial day, and Nate saw that the mud covered half an acre, maybe more. He saw something else, too.

Fifteen feet away was the black bear. It, too, had been caught in the mud, and at the moment seemed too bewildered to do anything. Then its head turned and it saw him, and a ferocious roar rent the storm.

Again Nate tried to pull free but his legs felt as if they weighed tons. The mud was like glue, impossibly strong glue, and the best he could do was lift one leg a few inches.

The bear was in a fury. Maybe it was the mud, or maybe it thought he was to blame somehow for it being caught in the muck. In any event, it roared and thrashed and tore at the mud in a berserker rage, and it made headway. Incredibly, slowly, inexorably, the black bear was moving toward him.

Nate looked for the others but they were nowhere to be seen. Even if they were close by, there was nothing they could do. They couldn't wade into the mud to help him or it would ensnare them, too.

The bear was clawing steadily closer.

Wedging the Hawken to his shoulder, Nate sighted down the barrel. He didn't have a clear heart or lung shot, and bear skulls were so thick, lead balls often glanced off. So he would shoot it in the eye. Thumbing back the hammer, he braced his arms against the wind and took a deep breath to steady his aim, then curled his forefinger around the trigger.

The bear was snapping and gnashing at the mud as if it was a flesh and blood adversary.

Except when lightning lit the scene, all Nate saw was a vague mass. As he soon found, trying to fix a bead on one of the bear's eyes was like trying to fix a bead on a pea in a dark room. A pea that was bobbing and twisting and dipping. In other words, it couldn't be done.

By now the bear was only ten feet away. Nate kept hoping it would stand still at the same moment lightning flared, but he hoped in vain. The bear was determined to reach him and wouldn't stop until his lifeless form was firmly gasped in its iron jaws. As for the storm, it showed no sign of abating any time soon.

Nate had to do something. Once the bear was within reach, he would be shredded to ribbons. He sighted on the center of its head, and at the next lightning flash, he stroked the trigger.

Nothing happened.

The Hawken had misfired. Nate thumbed back the hammer and squeezed the trigger again with the same result. Either the rain or the mud or both had rendered the rifle useless. It was doubtful his pistols would fire, either, since they were both covered by mud. That left his Bowie knife and his tomahawk, but against a bear that size, he might as well throw stones as try to stab it in the heart or split its skull.

The black bear was only eight feet away. The closer it came, the more frenzied its efforts became to reach him.

Nate couldn't reload, either, not with his ammo pouch

under the mud. And even if he managed to get some powder down the barrel, the driving rain would render it too wet to ignite.

Seven feet separated them now, and Nate didn't need the lightning to see the bear's bared fangs or the sweep of its mud-caked paws. He threw himself backward, trying to put distance between them. It was like trying to wade through a bog or quicksand, only the mud was a lot thicker. He moved first one leg and then the other, the mud impeding him to the point that it was soon apparent the bear would reach him in the next minute or two.

And all the time, the rain battered him and the wind tore at him and thunder boomed without a letup.

Nate strained his sinews to their utmost, forcing his right leg forward, then his left. He could hear the rasp of the bear's heavy breathing, could hear the smack of its paws on the mud. Taking hold of the Hawken by the barrel, he faced his pursuer. If it was his time to die, he would die fighting.

Suddenly the bear stopped and heaved onto its rear legs and spread its forelegs wide as bears did when they intended to catch prey in a viselike hug from which there was no escape.

Nate picked that moment to swing. He put his shoulders and all his weight into the blow and the Hawken's stock caught the black bear full across the lower jaw, a blow that would have downed most men in their tracks. But all the bear did was rear back and roar. Nate swung again, hoping the rifle's greater reach would enable him to hold the enraged carnivore at bay. This time he merely clipped it but that was enough to incite another maddened bellow of pain and rage.

The bear tried to advance on two legs but it had the same problem Nate did; it couldn't make headway. In its haste it nearly upended, and as it stood swaying and attempting to recover its balance, Nate swung the Hawken a third time. The stock thudded against bone above the bear's eye, and a yowl was ripped from the bear's throat and rose to the heavens.

Nate gripped the barrel anew and set himself. So far he was holding his own but all he was doing was inflicting a few bumps and bruises and feeding the bear's bloodlust. Eventually it would reach him, and when it did, the outcome was inevitable.

For a few seconds the thunder died. Nate thought he heard his name being shouted, but when he looked, he didn't see anyone.

"Winona? I'm over here!"

The bear took his cry as a challenge and issued a guttural cry of its own. An abrupt lunge brought it within striking range.

Nate ducked under an arcing paw and retaliated by driving the rifle into the bear's gut. It was akin to slamming the rifle into a solid wall. Bears always looked fat but they were masses of solid muscle.

All the black bear did was grunt.

A paw streaked at Nate's chest but the raking claws missed him by the width of a cat's whisker. He whipped the Hawken, smashing the bear under the jaw, and this time he landed a solid enough blow to cause the bear to stagger back. Or it would have, were it not for the mud. It only managed a shuffling step, then toppled like a tree felled by lumberjacks.

For a heartbeat Nate thought the mud would swallow

it as a wave swallowed a swimmer, but he had no such luck. The bear twisted and rose on all fours, caked brown from muzzle to hindquarters.

Again Nate tried to put distance between them. He realized he could see a bit better than before. The rain had slackened a little and lightning wasn't lancing the firmament every five seconds, but the storm was far from over. He took a partial step, then another, the mud begrudging him every inch.

The bear sensed that its triumph was near and gave a loping bound. Its claws clipped a sleeve on Nate's shirt.

Spinning, Nate struck the bear twice in succession on the forehead. He never saw its foreleg move but suddenly his Hawken went flying from his hands. Defenseless, he watched the black bear rear onto its hind legs once more. Now it was close enough to embrace him and there was nothing he could do.

Nate went to plunge a hand into the mud to grab hold of his tomahawk. Just then a strange thing happened. Feathers sprouted at the base of the bear's throat. It took a moment for it to register that the feathers were attached to an arrow, and by then a second shaft had found its mark in the bear's barrel body.

"Can you reach us, my husband?"

The edge of the mud wasn't more than thirty feet away. Just past it were Winona, Evelyn and Touch The Clouds, the giant Shoshone with another arrow notched to his bow string.

"Come on, Pa!" Evelyn shouted. "You can do it!"

Nate wished he had her confidence. They were close, so tantalizingly close, but the bear was closer and it was tearing through the mud as if they were in a race to a finish line.

For every two steps the bear took, though, it lost another. The mud was so slick, it couldn't help slipping and sliding.

"Hurry, Pa!" Evelyn hollered. "It's almost got you!"

Nate could see that for himself.

Two more shafts sank into the bear about where its vitals should be, but the bear kept on coming.

Nate raised his right leg to take another step but the mud was like a blanket wrapped tight. He teetered and would have fallen had he not flung his arms out from his sides for balance, and stopped dead.

The bear's next growl was practically in his ear.

Winona's rifle cracked, then the much smaller rifle Nate once had custom-made for his daughter. He swore he heard the *thwack* of lead against the bear's hide, but the shots had no more effect than the arrows.

Another moment, and the mud seemed to offer less resistance than before. Nate took a long stride, then a second. Thanks to the rain, the mud was thinning to the consistency of soup. He redoubled his effort to get clear of it before the bear overtook him.

Then some drops got into Nate's eyes, blurring his sight, and as he blinked to clear them, he inadvertently slowed. Not much, but it was enough. A blow to his back propelled him face-first into the muck. He swallowed mud as excruciating pain racked him. Levering an arm, he rose, but now he couldn't see a thing. Mud plastered his head and face.

"Pa!" Evelyn screamed.

"Look out!" Winona cried.

Frantically, Nate wiped at his eyes with his sleeve but it, too, was coated with mud. He raised his face to the rain and swiped at his eyes, and his vision cleared enough for him to see an enormous shape loom.

Iron teeth sheared into Nate's shoulder. Somehow his right hand found the hilt of his Bowie and he buried the blade in the black bear's neck, but its teeth held fast and the bear shook him as a terrier might shake a rabbit. Something warmer than the mud was trickling down his chest.

Suddenly Nate had the impression someone else was there. Blows were landing, but not his. He glimpsed Touch The Clouds, swinging a tomahawk. The pressure on his shoulder eased as the black bear turned to confront this new menace.

"Run, Grizzly Killer!" the giant Shoshone shouted.

Like hell, Nate thought, and stabbed the bear again, lower down. A paw caught him across the chest, spinning him halfway around. He thought his ribs had caved in but that didn't stop him from turning and stabbing the bear again and again and again, stabbing its neck and stabbing its shoulders and stabbing it in the side, stabbing and stabbing and stabbing until his arm ached so much he could barely lift it to stab again.

Belatedly, Nate became aware of a firm hand on his wrist and a voice saying something in the Shoshone tongue in his ear.

"—dead, Grizzly Killer! You have killed it!"

Nate blinked, and sure enough, the black bear was a motionless brown mound, blood oozing from a dozen wounds.

"Are you all right, my brother?" Touch The Clouds asked.

"Yes," Nate said, and smiled. He turned and took a step toward Winona and Evelyn, and that was as far as he got. The world faded to black, and the last sensation he experienced was that of falling into a bottomless void.

Chapter Twelve

Stanley P. Dagget was no fool. He knew Louisa King was up to something, he just didn't know what. She had been acting strangely ever since he picked her up. Several times he noticed how she moved her legs in a stiff-jointed fashion, as if they were sore or not working as they should.

Now, as Stanley followed Louisa and Zach King toward a small building across the parade ground, he watched them closely without letting on that he was doing so.

Sergeant Rotowski was ahead of them. Four soldiers followed, their rifles at the ready, taking no chances with their prisoner.

"I thank you again, Sergeant, for finding us a suitable room," Stanley said out of courtesy.

"Don't thank me, thank the colonel," was Rotowski's surly reply. "If it were up to me you'd do your talkin' in the breed's cell, and to hell with the three of you."

They had to go slowly because Zach was hampered by his shackles. Oddly enough, Stanley noticed that Lou was also taking short, slow steps. It looked like she was keeping pace with her husband but Stanley suspected there was more to it. She was favoring one of her legs, as if she had pulled a muscle. He considered asking her about it but decided doing so would alert her to his suspicion.

The building was a small auxiliary office, seldom used. There was a desk and a couple of chairs and a row of cabinets.

"My men will be right outside so don't get any brainstorms," Rotowski warned Zach King. "They're under orders to shoot to kill."

"That will be all, thank you," Stanley said, claiming the desk. "I'll send word when I'm finished. But it won't be for quite a while."

"Take all night, why don't you," Sergeant Rotowski said, and slammed the door after him.

"Nice man," Lou remarked.

"Why don't the two of you take seats," Stanley suggested. "We have a lot to cover if I'm to prepare an adequate defense."

Zach King held his wrists out. "Any chance you can have these bracelets taken off?"

"I'm sorry, but as I told you back at the stockade, there are limits to how much I can demand. We must adhere to army regulations whether we like them or not."

Zach sat down but Lou moved to the window and parted the curtains. "You would think two soldiers would be enough to guard us."

"What difference does it make?" Stanley responded. "It's not as if we're going anywhere."

"I reckon you're right." Lou smiled and sat next to her husband. "So where do we begin?"

For the better part of an hour Stanley quizzed Zachary

King, learning all he could. King wasn't talkative by nature, so at times extracting the facts was as difficult as prying open the lid on a warped cedar chest.

"I've made a list of the pertinent events," Stanley said at the conclusion, "and I would like to run them by you to be certain I have the sequence straight in my head. Are you agreeable?"

"Whatever it takes," Zach said.

"Artemis Borke and six other men established a trading post in Shoshone country during the first week of April," Stanley recited. "It was not long after this that some of the younger Shoshones took to drinking and staying out to all hours, and two Crows tried to kill the Shoshone leader, Touch The Clouds, with rifles from the trading post. Is that correct so far?"

"They killed others," Zach said. "Friends of mine."

"Of which you were unaware until you arrived in the Green River country to obtain herbal medicine from a Shoshone healer. You learned that the traders were inciting the Crows against the Shoshones, and you agreed to help the Shoshones drive the traders off."

"I did more than agree to help. I was the leader of the war party. The whole thing was my idea. And I wasn't out to drive the traders off, I was out to kill them."

Stanley frowned. "I respect your candor. But when it comes time for you to take the stand, you're to say exactly what I tell you."

"In other words, you want me to lie."

"Think of it more as a creative stretching of the truth." Stanley grinned but neither of the Kings appreciated his humor. "Tell me something. Weren't you the least concerned about the potential repercussions?"

"You mean, did I worry about other whites finding out?" Zach shook his head. "I burned the post to the ground and left Crow arrows all over so if anyone came to investigate, the Crows would be blamed."

"I see. You had no idea that a gentleman named Jacob Hyde had witnessed the whole affair?"

"Gentleman, hell. Hyde was as low a polecat as you'll find anywhere."

"In any event, to the best of your remembrance, the attack took place sometime between the second and tenth of May, correct?"

Zach shrugged. "I don't have much use for calendars."

Consulting his notes, Stanley said, "Hyde then sought out Borke's brother, Phineas, who immediately filed a formal complaint with the army. Lieutenant Pickforth was assigned to investigate, and he took you into custody after you slew Phineas Borke for abducting your wife to get at you."

"That's pretty much the whole story." Lou joined their conversation. "And here we are, twiddling our thumbs while the government tightens a noose around my husband's neck."

"Have faith, Mrs. King," Stanley tried to cheer her.

"I have more than faith."

Stanley wondered why, without any explanation, she suddenly bent down out of sight below the front of the desk. He was about to rise to see what she was doing when she straightened, holding a derringer in one hand and a dagger in the other. The derringer was pointed at him. "What is the meaning of this?"

"All this gum flapping isn't getting us anywhere. I'm

taking my husband out of here, Stanley, and I don't advise you to try and stop us."

"So this is why you've been behaving so oddly," Stanley said. "Put those down before you make a mistake you'll regret the rest of your life."

"My only mistake was in not shooting Lieutenant Pickforth the day I set eyes on that lecher." Standing, Lou sidled to the window and peeked out. "They're leaning on their rifles, bored out of their minds."

His chains clanking, Zach King rose.

"Please," Stanley said. "Hear me out before you do anything rash. All I ask is five minutes of your time."

"We've already wasted too much as it is," Lou said, giving the derringer to her husband.

Stanley had never met a pair like these two. Fearless to the point of reckless, wild to the point of lawless, they acted as if they had a perfect right to take the law into their hands whenever it suited their purpose. "Do you honestly think the two of you will make it out of the fort alive? Soldiers are everywhere."

"We'll take our chances," Lou defiantly replied.

"Are you that desperate?" Stanley challenged her. "Granted, I don't blame you for not trusting the army. But I doubt they'll repeat their folly in the exercise yard. It would arouse too much suspicion."

Lou stepped close to the door. "Says you. And even if you're right, you know as well as I do that we don't stand a prayer in court. Most folks are presumed innocent until they're found guilty. My Zach is presumed guilty until they find him guilty."

"What if I could get the sentence reduced to a prison term?"

"I told you before. My husband wouldn't last a year."

Zach nodded. "She's right." He jiggled the shackles on his wrists. "Do you have any idea what this is like for a person like me?"

"I can imagine," Stanley assured him.

"Can you? Can you really? To city dwellers, who spend most of their time indoors, a jail isn't much different from all the other rooms they spend their time in. They're used to being cooped up. But to a man like me, who hasn't been penned in a day in his life, it's torture."

"I sympathize. Sometimes we must grit our teeth and bear the hardships life has to offer as best we're able."

"Easy for you to say when you're not the one gritting his teeth," Zach rebutted. He pointed the derringer. "I want you to step to the door and tell those soldiers out there to fetch Sergeant Rotowski."

"Why?" Stanley asked.

"He has the keys. Don't let on that anything is wrong. I'll be holding this gun on you the whole time."

Stanley stayed where he was. "And if I refuse?"

"I don't want to hurt you but I will if I have to," Zach said. "It's my life that's at stake."

"That goes double for me," Lou piped up. "He's not going back to that miserable cell. I'll be damned if I'll let them go on caging him like some animal."

Rising, Stanley came around the desk. "I'll help you, but I'll do it under protest. If you're caught this will only make things worse. They'll pile more charges on top of those already leveled against you."

"Let them," Zach said. "Their charges won't mean a thing when we reach the mountains."

Louisa grinned. "We'll go so deep into the wilderness,

they'll never catch us. To a part of the Rockies no white man has ever gone before."

"And live the rest of your lives in hiding?" Stanley said. "Deprived of your family, of your friends, of all the people you've ever known? You'll be outcasts with a price on your heads. What sort of future is that?"

"Quit trying to tie our thoughts into knots and do as we told you," Lou said, pressing the dagger to his side.

Stanley was convinced she would use it if he gave her cause. She was a hellion, a fitting wife for her untamed mate. He opened the door partway, and when the soldiers turned, told them, "I need to see the sergeant, if one of you would be so kind."

"I'll fetch him," a corporal offered.

Stanley closed the door and stepped back. "I guess what surprises me the most about this is that I never took you two for cowards."

"What are you talking about?" Lou demanded. "The yellow thing to do is let them go on riding roughshod over us."

"The truly brave thing would be to beat them at their own game. To meet them in court and win. To stand up to them before the whole world."

"Win?" Zach snorted. "Against a stacked deck?"

"In the arena of law there are always loopholes," Stanley said. "All a good lawyer has to do is find them."

Lou had stepped to the window to keep an eye on the guards. Now she faced him and bluntly said, "Look me in the eye, lawyer-man, and give me your word that if we let the government put my husband on trial, you can convince the jury he's innocent."

"I can't," Stanley admitted.

"I figured as much," Lou said, and glanced at her husband and rolled her eyes to the ceiling.

Tense moments ensued. Stanley tried desperately to think of a way to talk them out of attempting to escape but logic alone wouldn't work. They weren't thinking with their heads, they were thinking with their hearts. He considered shouting to alert the troopers outside but decided not to; he would lose what little trust the Kings had extended to him, and might only succeed in getting them shot.

At last Lou announced, "Here comes the sergeant." To Stanley she said, "Ask him to come in. And remember. His life is in your hands." She flattened against the wall while Zach moved behind the door.

Stanley opened it. Rotowski had been about to knock. "Sergeant. Good of you to come so quickly."

"Save your insults, mister. The colonel said I was to cooperate. That doesn't include kissing your ass." Rotowski stared past him. "I take it you're done with the breed and we can take him back to his cell?"

"There are a few things I would like to discuss with you," Stanley said, stepping back. "Come in, if you would."

Sergeant Rotowski shouldered the door open. "This had better be impor—" he began, then froze, because by then Zach had closed the door and pressed the derringer to his head and Lou was holding the dagger against his ample belly.

"The keys," Zach growled.

Lou lowered the dagger below his belt. "Or do I cut off something near and dear to you?"

Rotowski's thick lips moved but no sounds came out.

"Call for your men if you want," Zach said, "but it will be the last thing you ever do."

"Damn you to hell," Sergeant Rotowski hissed, and glared at Stanley. "Are you in this with them?"

"He's being made to help, just like you," Lou said, and to accent her point, she jabbed the sergeant's groin. Not hard enough to pierce his pants or his privates, but it had the desired result.

"The keys are in my shirt pocket."

Lou swiftly unlocked her husband's shackles, and once he was free, the first thing Zach King did was enfold her in his left arm and hug her close. "God, I've missed you. I don't ever want to be apart again."

"We won't be," Lou pledged.

Rotowski made a sound reminiscent of a goat being strangled. "I can't wait to slap those irons back on and then find a matching set for you, you breed-lovin' witch."

Livid with anger, Zach spun the sergeant around and jammed the derringer against his cheek. "Order two of your men to come in. One wrong word, one wrong look, and I repay you for all the times you've kicked and hit me."

Stanley tried a final time. "It's still not too late to change your minds. No one has been harmed. Mrs. King might get off lightly. But once we're out that door, there's no telling what will happen. I'm begging you. Please reconsider."

The Kings looked at one another. Lou grinned and nodded, and Zach took a step to the right so he couldn't be seen when the door was opened. "Let's get this over with."

Chapter Thirteen

Shakespeare McNair sometimes wondered why it was that two people fell in love. Out of the thousands of others a person met in life, why was it that one, in particular, filled the human heart with more happiness than it could contain? He had loved Blue Water Woman practically from the day he first set eyes on her, yet try as he might, he couldn't find the words to express why. What was it about her, of all the women in the world, that drew him to her and forged an emotional bond stronger than the strongest metal?

Usually when Shakespeare waxed philosophical, he turned to William S. or the Good Book, and one or the other or both had the answer he sought. But when it came to the essence of love, both were lacking. Oh, the Bard had penned verse after verse about the beauty and the wonder and the tragedy of love, but nowhere was love defined in its purest terms. In the Bible it said that God created the first man and first woman and commanded them to be fruitful and multiply, which, while it certainly must have pleased Adam, didn't explain what love was. Even the Song of Solomon, the naughtiest account of love Shakespeare ever read, bubbled on about thighs like jewels and navels like goblets and not on the underlying love that brought lovers together.

Personally, Shakespeare liked to think of love as a miracle. What with all the evil and ugliness and violence in the world, the fact that two people could open their hearts to each other, open them fully and completely and with total and pure trust, was a miracle of the highest order.

He never ceased to be amazed by Blue Water Woman's love for him. It astounded him that a woman so lovely and intelligent and fine should be smitten by so coarse and frisky a character. He wasn't easy to live with. A man of strong habits and stronger opinions, he could be as cantankerous as an old moose. Yet love him she did.

Once, when strolling along the lake near Nate King's cabin, little Evelyn had asked, "Uncle Shakespeare, how do you know when you're in love?"

Without any hesitation, Shakespeare responded, "When you are willing to do anything for the other person."

"But I'll do anything for you or Ma or Pa."

Shakespeare had grinned down at her. "Would you jump off a cliff if I asked you to?"

"Of course not. That would be stupid."

"Then you don't love me as much as you'll one day love the boy who claims your heart, because if he asked you to, you would."

"That's plain silly," Evelyn said.

"Maybe so, but no one ever claimed love was sane."

Evelyn had laughed, thinking he was joking, but Shakespeare had never been more in earnest in his life. Two people were truly in love when they were willing to do anything for each other, anything at all.

There was more to love, of course, but in Shakespeare's estimation, that was the distilled essence he had long sought. Or would serve as the essence until a better explanation came along.

He thought of this now as he gazed across the trail by

the Platte River at the tree behind which Blue Water Woman was crouched. She was a marvel, that gal. Half the time she seemed to know what his thoughts were as he was thinking them, and the other half she thought them before he did. She was part of him, heart, soul, mind and body, and he wouldn't have it any other way.

Blue Water Woman noticed him staring, and smiled. Shakespeare grinned like an idiot and would have waved but just then several riders materialized to the west. It was the trio they had been waiting for, one bent low over his saddle, his shirt off, his chest crisscrossed with crude bandages.

Shakespeare waited until they were barely twenty feet away, then strode to the middle of the trail, and beamed. "Morning, gents. I hear tell you're interested in getting your hands on my poke?"

They drew rein, their surprise quickly replaced by wary suspicion.

"You!" the one in the middle blurted, and scanned both sides of the trail. "What the hell do you think you're doing, poppin' out on us like that?"

"I wanted to play peek-a-boo and you were the only kids I could find."

"You're loco, do you know that? You and your crazy friend. Where is he, by the way? Waitin' in ambush along with that redwood of an Injun?"

"Been to California, I see," Shakespeare commented. "But no, my friends have gone on ahead. Take heart, however." He quoted the Bard: "They praise you, and make an ass of you. Now your foes tell you plainly that you are an ass, so that by your foes, sir, you profit in the knowledge of yourself."

"That was an insult."

"I'll never believe a madman until I see his brains," Shakespeare quoted, and shifted so he could watch the one on the left better. The man's hand was on his hip, an inch from a pistol.

"Madman? Me? You're the one spoutin' insanity."

Shakespeare placed a hand to his chest and dipped his head in mock salute. "My compliments, sir. Your wit far exceeds expectations." He sobered and said, "Now then, to the business at hand. My wife would as soon shoot you but that won't be necessary if we can strike a deal."

"Old man, if you ever make sense, the shock will kill me."

"That's twice now!" Shakespeare exclaimed. "You're getting better by the moment. But let's talk turkey. We want your horses."

"You what?"

"Two, to be exact. One of ours had the misfortune of going lame and the other had the bad luck of having a lightning bolt take a shine to it and passed on to greener pastures on high."

"You're worse than loco. You're a gibberin' idiot."

"That's the spirit!"

"If you think my brothers and me are going to hand our horses over to you, you old buzzard, you have another think or three comin'."

Shakespeare chuckled. He was enjoying himself immensely. "And you accuse me of not making any sense?" He paused. "What's your handle, by the way?"

"Ziphion. Why?"

"Ziphion?"

"Our folks were real biblical."

"My condolences. If I went through life with a name like that, I'd be as big a grouch as you."

Ziphion lifted his reins. "Enough of this childishness. Get out of our way, or so help me, we'll ride you down where you stand."

"I'd rather do the riding," Shakespeare responded. "So why not be magnanimous and spare everyone a few pints of blood?"

"I don't even know what that word means," Ziphion said, then virtually screamed, "Now get the hell out of our way!"

"How much for two horses?"

Ziphion looked at his brothers and then at the sky and then back at Shakespeare. "I don't believe you. I honestly don't. You must have solid granite between your ears. You can't have our mounts at any price, numbskull."

"Not even for half my gold?"

"What?"

"You wanted to get your hands on my poke. I'm offering you the chance to have half of it for two of your critters. It's important my wife and I reach Fort Leavenworth without delay."

"Half your poke?" Ziphion licked his lips. "How much would that be, do you reckon? A couple of hundred?"

"More like a thousand," Shakespeare exaggerated.

The brother on the left cleared his throat. "We can't do it, Ziph. We dug the slugs out of brother Caleb but he still needs doctorin'."

"You hush up, brother Onan."

"Onan?" Shakespeare said. "Wasn't he the one who—"

"You can hush, too," Ziphion snapped, and glanced at each of his brothers. "Listen good. A thousand dollars is more than any of us have ever had. Hell, it's more than anyone in our family has ever had, and our folks say our line goes clear back to Moses."

"I sure would like to meet those parents of yours one day," Shakespeare couldn't resist remarking.

Ziphion paid him no heed. "A thousand dollars is a fortune. Why, when we split it three ways, it comes to . . ." He stopped, his brow puckering. "It comes to . . ." He began ticking off the amounts on his fingers. "It comes to . . ."

"Three hundred and thirty-three dollars apiece," Shakespeare helped him. "You can flip a coin for the extra dollar."

"What I don't get," Onan said, "is why we just don't rub this old fart out and take all his gold?"

"Because," Ziphion replied, "he wouldn't be dumb enough to waltz out in the open like this unless someone had a rifle on us."

"I'm so proud of you I could bust," Shakespeare said. He patted his possibles bag. "So do we have a deal? If it will make you feel better, my wife will take a look at Caleb. She has some Flathead medicine that might help."

"Injun stuff?" Onan said. "I don't want nothin' to do with heathen concoctions."

"You're not the one who was shot," Shakespeare reminded him.

"Our ma says Injuns dabble with the devil," Onan declared. "She says their medicine men can turn themselves into coyotes and the like."

"Your mother is more remarkable than I imagined. But all my wife will do is sprinkle some powder on Caleb's wounds to help them heal."

"She won't turn him into a raven or a snake or anything like that?"

"Not unless you want her to."

The brothers whispered among themselves. Then Ziphion and Onan dismounted, helped Caleb down, and sat him with his back to a tree.

"There will be no tendin' him until we have our gold," Ziphion declared.

"A man should always have his priorities straight," Shakespeare said, and motioned. Blue Water Woman came from concealment, her rifle trained on the threesome. While she watched them, Shakespeare opened his possibles bag, took out his pouch, and gave half his remaining nuggets to Ziphion.

The brothers were dazzled by the glittering ore. Even Caleb, who reverently fingered one and breathed, "Lordy! Look at how it shines. This here is the prettiest thing I ever saw."

"We only need one of your saddles," Shakespeare said. His was a few yards off the trail.

Ziphion had taken the largest nugget and held it up to the sunlight. The sparkle of pure greed was in his eyes. "I've always dreamed of havin' me some gold. Mountains and mountains of it."

Shakespeare took his turn covering them while his wife sank onto a knee beside Caleb. From a beaded pouch she produced a small glass bottle plugged by a cork, then reached for one of Caleb's bandages.

"What in tarnation do you reckon you're doing, squaw?" he demanded.

"The powder has to go directly on your wounds, boy,"

Shakespeare explained, overlooking, for the moment, the slight to his wife.

Caleb tapped the bottle Blue Water Woman held. "What's in there, anyhow? It's not lizard guts or owl's eyes or anything like that?"

Blue Water Woman answered. "It is a powder made from plantain leaves, as whites call them, mixed with honeysuckle root."

"Dang," Caleb said. "You speak English better than me." He held the bottle to his nose, and even though the cork was still in, sniffed it a few times. "You swear this stuff won't do me harm?"

"She's used it on me many a time," Shakespeare related. "Indians have medicines for all sorts of ailments. Juniper for rheumatism, toza for the heart, elderberry for inflammation. You name it, they have a cure."

"Can't she just give me some so I can put it on myself?" Caleb requested. "I ain't never been half-naked in front of a female. Ma would take a switch to our backsides if she ever caught us without all our clothes on, or she'd have Pa do it."

"Sure, we can give you some of the powder," Shakespeare said. Only then did he notice Ziphion and Onan had moved off half a dozen yards and were whispering in each other's ears. Ziphion glanced at his possibles bag, so it wasn't hard for Shakespeare to guess what they were talking about. "Damn," he said softly. Leaning his rifle against the tree, he folded his arms across his chest, his fingertips brushing his pistols.

"I hope the medicine helps with the pain," Caleb was saying. "I've been hurting something awful."

"Many a barb we must bear while in this mortal coil,"

Shakespeare said. "Most of them self-inflicted in one form or another."

"I didn't understand a lick of that," Caleb confessed.

Shakespeare bobbed his chin at the other two brothers. "Foul devils, for God's sake, hence, and trouble us not. For thou hast made the happy earth thy hell, filled it with cursing cries and deep exclaims. If thou delight to view thy heinous deeds, behold this pattern of thy butcheries."

"What are you sayin'?" Caleb asked.

"You blocks, you stones, you worse than senseless things." Shakespeare raised his voice. "Be content with what you have."

"Ziphion?" Caleb said.

The older brothers had chosen their course. Side by side, they spun. Side by side, they brought up their rifles. And side by side they were shot squarely through their chests. Onan buckled at the knees, his inner ghost fled before he struck the ground. Ziphion gawked at the hole in his sternum, then at the smoking flintlocks in Shakespeare's hands. He wound up side-by-side with Onan.

"No!" Caleb cried, and clawed at one of his own pistols.

Blue Water Woman was faster. Snatching it from under his belt, she clubbed him over the head and he sagged like an empty sack of flour.

"Getting soft in your old age?" Shakespeare bantered.

"I could not shoot him. He is so young." Blue Water Woman opened the bottle. "Help me, and we can be on our way."

Shakespeare faced east. "I just hope we get there in time."

Chapter Fourteen

Nate King dreamed he was in a cave. He could feel the cold, clammy walls with his outstretched hands but he couldn't see anything. It was black as pitch. He felt he had to get out of there and sensed a great danger lurking in the dark. Something unseen, awaiting its moment to pounce. Growing frantic, he stumbled blindly along. Again and again he bumped a shin or a knee against rock outcroppings and was lanced by pain.

Then Nate heard a voice, so faint at first, he thought his ears were deceiving him. By gradual degrees it grew louder and soon he realized someone was calling a name over and over. His name, he discovered, and he moved faster, spurred by the thought that if he didn't find the source of that voice, and soon, he would never see the light of day again.

Nate ran, or tried to. Stumbling and careening off the cave walls, he rounded turn after turn. The voice grew clearer. It was a woman, and she was saying his name so tenderly, so lovingly, that his heart ached to be with her. He heard himself saying, "Winona? Winona?" And then his eyes blinked open and he squinted against the glare of the afternoon sun and beheld his wife's lovely face floating above him.

"I am here, husband." Winona kissed him on the lips and ran a hand through his hair. "You gave us quite a scare."

"You sure did," Evelyn's face appeared beside her mother's, both of them smiling yet apprehensive.

"Where—" Nate raised his head and saw the broken bluff and the mud slide a goodly distance away. He lay in a clearing near the river, naked except for a blanket over him. "My clothes?"

"Are hanging on a branch to dry." Winona pointed at a tree. "They were caked with mud. We had to wash them."

"The bear?" Nate said, as it all came back to him in a harrowing rush of fangs and claws.

"Touch The Clouds is skinning it as we speak. He did not want the hide to go to waste." Winona placed a hand on his forehead. "You have a slight fever from your wounds."

Nate lifted the blanket. A different one had been cut into strips and his shoulder, upper chest and lower ribs bandaged. "How bad am I?"

"No bones were broken, as near as I can tell. The worst is your back. The bear's claws opened you up from your shoulder blades to your hip."

Now that she mentioned it, Nate felt something wadded underneath him.

"It nearly severed your spine." Winona clasped his hand to her bosom. "A bit deeper and you would never move your legs again."

"But I still can?" Nate said, and confirmed it by moving both his feet a few inches. "As soon as my clothes are dry, we're lighting a shuck for Fort Leavenworth."

"No, husband, we are not."

"Zach needs us. He goes on trial soon. I can't let something like this slow us down."

"I am sorry. I love Stalking Coyote as much as you and I dearly want to be with him, but you can not ride for a few days, if then, or you risk infection setting in."

Nate seldom argued with her. They almost always saw eye-to-eye. But now he declared, "I'll be damned if I'll leave our son in the lurch when he needs us most."

"The wounds on your back are too severe for you to go anywhere." Winona squeezed his good shoulder. "Trust me. Have I ever lied to you?"

"I'm going, and that's final." Nate lay his head down. He wanted to roar like the black bear had, he was so mad. Not at her. At Fate. At the cruel injustice of it all. They needed to be there for Zach's trial so they could speak in his defense. It was up to them to explain to the jury how things were and why their son had done what he did.

"There is more," Winona said. "We have not found your horse yet. We are hoping it will return on its own. If not, Touch The Clouds has offered to go after it."

"If it doesn't come back, I'll ride double with one of you," Nate proposed.

"I keep forgetting how stubborn you can be."

Nate grinned to try and lighten her mood. "I hear tell most men are the same. Not that you women are ever hardheaded." He chuckled, and was suddenly racked by excruciating agony, agony so potent, he groaned and nearly doubled over.

"Now will you believe me when I say you are in a bad way?" Winona asked. "If you try to ride before your back has sufficiently healed, you might die."

Evelyn had been content to listen but now she said, "Do as she says, Pa. Please. We can see your insides through the cuts in your back."

"They're that deep?" The gravity of his wounds sank in, and Nate grit his teeth to keep from using language he never used in front of his wife and daughter.

"We have a fire going," Winona mentioned, "and soon I will have a poultice to apply." She rose and moved off.

The sky had largely cleared but from the east came the boom of thunder. Nate twisted his head and saw the eastern horizon blotted out by the trailing edge of the storm front.

"I'm sorry you were hurt," Evelyn said, resting her cheek on his arm. "But you'll mend, given time."

"Time is the one thing we don't have to spare," Nate responded. "Not if we're to save your brother."

"Ma says the trial will take a good long while, so there's no rush."

Nate hadn't thought of that. Odds were, Winona was right. A trial of this order would take weeks, maybe even months. Maybe a few days's delay wasn't the calamity he thought it was, he mused.

"Why has all this happened?" Evelyn asked forlornly. "We didn't do anything to deserve it."

"No one hardly ever does," Nate said. "It's just how life is."

Evelyn peered skyward. "It's not right. Zach only did what he had to. Why did they have to go and drag him off like they did?"

"He broke the law. He killed white men."

"But you've killed white men. More than I can count. And the army never sent soldiers after you."

"I've only killed in self-defense or to protect those I care for," Nate justified his actions. "And the ones I killed were cutthroats and murderers."

"So were the men at the trading post. Vermin, you called them, who would have brought no end of trouble to the Shoshones."

"But the army doesn't know they were vermin. It's up to us to tell them," Nate said. But here he lay, mauled and helpless. His frustration was boundless.

"It's things like this that make me want to leave the mountains when I'm older," Evelyn mentioned. "I want to live in a city somewhere. A place where there aren't any vermin. Where I don't have to worry about a griz attacking me or hostiles wanting to take me captive every time I step outside."

"City life isn't the paradise you seem to think," Nate said, recalling his own early years in New York City. "It can be as dangerous as the wilderness."

"You're just saying that because Ma and you don't want me to go. But I'm tired of seeing blood spilled. I'm tired of only ever feeling safe when we're in our cabin with the door barred."

"City dwellers have to bar and lock their doors, too."

"But they don't need to be walking armories when they're outdoors," Evelyn countered. "Admit it. City life is a lot safer than life in the wilds."

"Not a lot," Nate said.

Evelyn pecked his chin. "Maybe so, but my mind is made up. But it's not as if you'll never see me again. I won't move that far away. St. Louis maybe, or New Orleans."

To Nate, either might as well be Jupiter. It was a given that, just like hatchlings, kids one day grew up and flew the nest, as his son already had. But Zach's cabin was only a few valleys to the north of his own. Evelyn was moving many hundreds of miles. To visit her would take weeks of travel. He would hardly ever get to see her again, and that saddened him immensely.

"I should think you would be happy for me."

"You do, huh?"

"Sure. Ma and you won't have to fret over me nearly as much. There aren't any mountain lions or rattlesnakes where I'm going."

"Some sidewinders wear pants." Nate set her straight and tenderly placed a hand on her head. "But you do what you want. Your mother and I won't stand in your way. There comes a time when everyone has to stand on their own two feet and make their own decisions."

Evelyn hugged him. "I knew I could count on you. Ma and you are the best parents anyone could have."

"If you say so." In Nate's view he had fallen a few notches short of the mark. When they were little, he had been away from home too often, either off trapping or exploring. Then there were all the times his family had been in peril. If he were truly the good father Evelyn thought, he'd have dragged them back to the States long ago.

Winona returned carrying one of their pots, from which steam was rising, and a clean cloth. She set them down, and knelt. "We must roll you over, husband. And I warn you, it will hurt."

"I can take it," Nate said, but he almost couldn't. The pain was far worse than he anticipated, pain so severe he bit his lower lip, and quaked. It subsided when he was flat on his stomach but it didn't fade entirely. He felt his wife remove the bandage and her fingers probe his back.

Sharp, stabbing agony suddenly pierced him, and he thought he would pass out.

"I am sorry," Winona said. "I needed to see how deep one of the cuts went."

"How deep?" Nate asked.

"You do not want to know."

Winona was as gentle as she could be but he still came within a thread's-width of screaming a few times. First she washed the wounds, then she spread the poultice, then she reapplied the bandage, tying it tight so it wouldn't slip. "There. All done," she informed him, sitting back.

Nate was slick with sweat but his body felt like ice. Never a good sign. "I want to be on my side."

"It is best if you do not move for a while."

Fatigue crept over him. Nate tried to stay awake but his eyes kept shutting. Five or six times he opened them again, his head bent so he could see Winona and Evelyn. But then came a time when they closed and he lost all sensation. He was out for hours. Stars sparkled in the firmament when he became conscious of the murmur of conversation, and of the ground under his cheek. Out of habit he started to rise and was spiked by more extreme torment.

In the blink of an eye Winona was at his side, her arm across his shoulders. "Do not try to get up. I will bring you something to eat and drink if you want."

Nate refused to eat lying down, refused to be spoon-fed like an invalid. "Sit me up."

"I would rather not."

"Bring a saddle, and have Touch The Clouds lift me," Nate insisted. When she hesitated, he placed his hands flat and started to push himself up. It shocked him how weak he was. All he could do was rise a few inches, then he had to lie back down.

"Please do not try that again," Winona pleaded. "My medicine can only do so much." She hastened to her saddle and brought it over.

"Touch The Clouds?" Nate said in the Shoshone tongue, twisting his head. The giant warrior appeared at his elbow, and Nate explained, finishing with, "Do it quick. But give me a stick first."

Winona and Evelyn hovered anxiously. Nate smiled to reassure them, then clamped his teeth on the stick. Touch The Clouds's fingers curled around his upper arms, and Touch The Clouds smiled.

"Are you ready, Grizzly Killer?"

Nate nodded. And just like that, it was done. Near-overwhelming pain speared through him and the world spun like a wagon wheel. Spitting out the stick, he sucked in breath and tried not to let on how much he was hurting. "That wasn't so bad."

"You are a terrible liar," Winona told him. Kneeling, she checked his forehead, then the bandages. "As I feared. You are bleeding again but I will wait a while before I apply new bandages." She nodded at the fire. "Would you like soup?"

The thought of food made Nate queasy but he wanted to give her the impression he was better off than she thought so he smiled and replied, "Soup and coffee, both."

A gust of wind caused Nate to shiver. He was about to ask for another blanket to cover himself but his daughter beat him to it and covered him on her own. He thanked her, then watched his wife ladle soup from the cook pot. "There's something I'd like you to do for me."

"Anything, husband."

"I want the three of you to go on without me."

Winona did not even look at him. "You ask the silliest things. That is out of the question."

"You just said you would do anything," Nate noted.

"Anything sensible, yes. Anything reasonable. But it is ridiculous to ask us to desert you when you are incapable of fending for yourself."

"I can manage."

"This from a man who cannot sit up on his own. You would not last three days. Forgive me for being selfish, but I have not devoted myself to you for so long only to lose you now."

"It's not about me, it's about our son. Head out at the crack of dawn and you should reach the fort in plenty of time."

"I am sorry. No."

"Damn it, Winona. Our boy's life comes before mine."

"That is not your decision to make."

"Like hell it isn't."

"I am your wife and his mother and I have a say in what we do. But this is not about choice. This is about doing what must be done." Winona brought his soup over, and Nate saw that her eyes were glistening with tears. "I will not abandon you. When you are fit enough to ride we will go on together, and not before."

In all the years of their marriage, Nate had never been so mad at her. "Then our son is as good as hung."

Chapter Fifteen

Zach King pressed the derringer to the back of Sergeant Rotowski's head and stood so the soldiers outside couldn't see him. "Remember, one wrong word and I splatter your brains all over creation." He almost wished Rotowski would give him an excuse to do it, after all the man had done.

"Don't worry, breed, I'll do what you want." Rotowski grinned. "Only because it won't do you any good. There's no way in hell you're getting off this post." He opened the door part way and gruffly barked, "Peterson, Isaacs, I need you in here."

The moment the pair filed inside, Lou closed the door and pressed her dagger to the neck of the last private to enter. The other trooper started to unsling his rifle but turned to stone when he saw Zach's derringer pressed against Rotowski's head.

"What's going on, Sarge?"

Rotowski was not one to suffer stupid questions. "You have eyes, you idiot. Use them. The bitch and the breed think they can escape."

Zach came close to squeezing the trigger. He couldn't abide insults to his wife, not under any circumstances. Commanding the sergeant to sit, he pointed the derringer at the first private and relieved him of his rifle. Then, stepping well back, he leveled the rifle and cocked it.

Lou had the other private's rifle. Neither private had

pistols but they did have ammo pouches and bayonets, which she relieved them of.

All the while, the lawyer hadn't said a word. Now he took a step toward Zach, saying, "I must stress yet again that you are making a grave mistake."

"Don't come any closer," Zach warned. "Sit at the desk and behave yourself." To Lou he said, "Watch them." He used the trooper's belts and strips he cut from their shirts with a bayonet to bind and gag them, then dragged them to a corner and sat them facing the wall.

"Call in the other two," Zach said, jamming the rifle's muzzle against Rotowski's midsection. "Same as before."

Privates were so accustomed to obeying their superiors without question that the second pair were as easy to take by surprise as the first. Zach made them strip off their uniforms, then bound them and hauled them to the corner. "Your turn," he told Rotowski.

Angrily extending his wrists, the sergeant muttered, "I can't wait for them to stretch your stinkin' neck. I'll be in the front row cheerin' them on."

"Good. You'll be the one I spit on as the noose tightens," Zach said, and slammed the rifle against Rotowski's ear. It burst like rotten flesh and Rotowski oozed to the floor. In a burst of excess hatred, Zach smashed the stock against him again and would have done it more times if not for Stanley P. Dagget.

"Stop! If you're not careful, you'll kill him."

Zach had had enough out of Dagget. He tied the lawyer to the chair, commenting, right before he stuffed a gag into his mouth, "No hard feelings? I'm only doing what I have to."

"Don't we all?" Dagget responded. "But don't worry.

I'll still represent you if you don't get away."

"Damned decent of you," Zach said as he tied the gag in place. He then bound and gagged Rotowski, and tossed one of the uniforms to Lou. "Put this on. The hat too, so it's not as obvious you're a woman."

"Why, I never thought you noticed," Lou said, and snickered.

The uniform Zach donned smelled of lye and starch and was much too stiff. Leave it to whites, he reflected, to wear such uncomfortable clothes. With the hat pulled low he could pass for a soldier if no one looked at him too closely. "We must hurry." Slinging his rifle, he glanced at his wife.

Lou had her back to the soldiers and was pulling the uniform on over her buckskins.

"What do you think you're doing? Someone will notice."

"This uniform is baggy enough, don't worry," Lou responded. "If you think I'm taking my buckskins off, think again."

That was why Zach had turned the soldiers and the lawyer to the wall. Shrugging, he said, "Whatever you want." He cracked the door and verified no one was in their immediate vicinity. "Stay close and keep your chin down." He glanced over his shoulder one last time just as Dagget turned his head and shook it vigorously to discourage them. The man just never gave up.

The cavalry had stopped drilling and the post was still. Zach turned right and hurried behind the office. Since there was no palisade, they could leave the post from any direction. All he had to do was watch for the sentries.

He headed west, toward the wide open prairie and freedom, hugging the buildings as much as possible. Lou was close behind him. Too close, for when he suddenly halted, she walked into him.

"Why did you stop like that?" Lou asked.

Zach pointed.

General Risher and Lieutenant Pickforth were over near the stockade. Risher said something to the lieutenant and they headed across the parade ground toward the auxiliary office.

"Of all the rotten luck!"

Zach walked faster. Another fifty to sixty yards and they would reach a stand of trees bordering the prairie. Once there they could lie low until dark and then head for the Rockies, and sanctuary. Never again would he let himself be caught. Never again would he let the whites put him behind bars.

General Risher, Zach noticed, was walking fast. It figured. Lou had mentioned luck. All his of late had been bad. It was just bad luck that the fight at the trading post had been witnessed by a white man. Just bad luck that the trading post owner had a brother every bit as evil and vicious as himself. Just bad luck that the army sent a patrol, and even worse luck that he had fallen into their hands.

Deep in thought, Zach came to the end of another building and nearly collided with someone coming around it.

"Watch where you're going there, Private."

It was an officer. A captain, Zach believed. He snapped to attention as he had seen other soldiers do. "Sorry, sir."

The captain took another step, then stopped. "Why is your hair so long? Regulations specifically state that—"

The captain's eyes widened and he blurted, "You! You're supposed to be in the stockade!"

By then Zach had his hands on his slung rifle and whipped the stock in an arc that connected with the captain's chin. Looking to be sure no one had seen, he rolled the unconscious officer against the building.

"They'll be on to us any second."

Zach did not need to be reminded. He bolted for the trees, Lou easily keeping pace. She was almost as fleet of foot as he was, and ran in long, graceful strides that always reminded him of a sleek antelope.

Shouts broke out when they still had twenty yards to go. Zach spotted a sentry to the north, his back to them. He pumped his legs, pouring on every last ounce of speed he had, and he and Lou gained cover just as the sentry turned to gaze across the post in the direction of the commotion.

Lou was panting and nearly out of breath. "That was close," she whispered.

The yells were spreading like wildfire. Soldiers were dashing this way and that. Crouched behind a maple, Zach saw General Risher bark orders and troopers scurry to obey.

Lieutenant Pickforth came out of the auxiliary building, Stanley P. Dagget on his heels. The lawyer was rubbing his wrists and the pair appeared to be arguing. After them came the four soldiers, supporting Sergeant Rotowski.

"I wish it was night," Lou said.

So did Zach. "As soon as the sun sets, we'll slip off across the plain." In the high grass they would be as hard to spot as prairie dogs.

The entire post was in an uproar. Every last soldier was

being called out, hundreds of them, and organized into search parties. Some went from building to building. Others searched clusters of vegetation like the one Zach and Lou were in. Cavalry troops were mounting up to sweep the prairie.

Lou crawled from her tree to Zach's and rose onto her knees to take one of his hands into both of hers. "If they catch us, I want you to know I'm sorry."

"For what?" Zach was thinking of the captain he had slugged; it would not be long before someone found him.

"For not planning this better. Maybe I should have waited until the trial, when there were fewer soldiers around."

"But plenty of others." Zach was watching the whirlwind of activity and was surprised when she pressed her cheek to his and her skin was damp. "You're crying?"

"I love you so much, Zachary King."

Zach kissed her and she responded with all the passion in her heart and soul. It was a kiss sweeter than honey, a kiss to end all other kisses. The kind of kiss that made a person feel warm all over. Neither of them were anxious for it to end. Their lips lingered in moist bliss until a shout from nearby brought Zach crashing down from the dizzying heights of rapture to the jagged rocks of reality.

The sentry he had seen, and another, were coming toward the trees.

Flattening, Zach gestured. With Lou at his elbow he crawled to the south end of the stand and they lay on their bellies behind the second-to-last tree. The trunk wasn't wide enough to screen them both so he whispered, "Climb on top of me." She nodded and eased up onto his back until her chin brushed his head and their bodies were flush.

"If they come close," she whispered, "I'll run off and draw them away from you."

"You'll do no such thing."

Lou lowered her lips to his left ear. "You're the one facing the gallows. The important thing is for you to escape."

"No."

"I'll doubt they'll do much to me. I'm a woman."

"No."

"What's the worst they can do? Sentence me to a year in prison?"

Zach shifted so he could see her face. "I could not bear the thought of you behind bars. If they see us, we will run off together, and if we are caught, we will be caught together."

"You're one romantic devil, do you know that?"

"Women," Zach grinned.

"Men," Lou said.

And then a twig crunched and they stiffened and Zach turned his head to see uniformed shapes flitting through the stand. The sentries were going from tree to tree, looking behind each one.

"They'll find us!" Lou whispered, and put her hands on his back to push to her feet and bolt.

"Stay put!" Zach growled. His rifle was next to his right arm, hers on the other side of him. He could shoot the sentries but the shots would bring every soldier at the fort down on their heads.

The pair had covered half the stand. Zach heard Lou's sharp intake of breath and reached behind him to grip her buckskins. He wouldn't put it past her to defy him and run, and he refused to allow her to make the sacrifice; the sentries might shoot her.

"There's nothing here, Frank," one of the men declared.

"Only a dozen more to check," Frank replied. He started toward a tree in a direct line with the maple Zach and Lou were behind, then abruptly stopped and wheeled and said, "You're right. We'd have seen them by now. Let's go."

Lou exhaled in relief into Zach's ear but Zach was troubled. He didn't like how the soldier suddenly turned like that.

"Another close shave," Lou whispered, sliding off. "Now all we do is wait for dark and we're gone."

The sentries emerged from the trees and Frank raised an arm and waved it back and forth.

Zach glanced at the prairie, so tantalizingly close, then at his wife. "Have I told you lately how much I love you?"

"And I, you." Lou snuggled against him and kissed his cheek. "I can't wait to have you back in the mountains and all to myself."

Over two dozen cavalrymen were trotting toward the sentries.

"I never thought I could care for anyone as deeply as I care for you," Lou whispered. "I figured I would end my days a spinster." She grinned. "Strange, the notions we get sometimes."

The cavalry reined up. A lieutenant said something to Frank, then leaned down to hear what Frank was saying.

"Life has a way of stripping us of our illusions," Lou had gone on. "We always think we're different from everyone else. We think the things that happen to them will never happen to us. But we're wrong."

Zach saw the lieutenant straighten and snap a crisp command at his men and jab his spurs. Some of the cavalrymen broke to the north, others to the south. He pulled Lou to him and kissed her again. The drum of hooves grew louder but he didn't look. He didn't need to. He knew what the soldiers were doing.

"Oh, my," Lou said when they parted for breath. "That was better than the first. You pretty near curled my toes."

"Thank you, Louisa, for trying to save me."

"Trying?" Lou said, and gave a start.

By then the cavalry had ringed the stand and were facing it with their rifles to their shoulders, except for the young lieutenant, who had drawn his saber.

"They know!" Lou exclaimed.

"They know."

"Why didn't you warn me? Why didn't we run?"

Zach didn't answer.

The lieutenant rose in his stirrups. "Zachary King! We know you and your wife are in there! Come out with your hands over your heads and you won't be harmed! Resist and we will cut you down!"

Lou snatched her rifle. "We have enough ammo to hold them off for a while."

"No." Zach knocked the rifle from her hands, seized her wrists, and stood, lifting her with him.

"Please!" Lou cried, struggling. "Haven't you always told me a warrior should go down fighting?"

"Not when the one who has claimed his heart will go down with him." His chest heavy, his throat constricted, Zach pulled her into the open and raised her arms with his. "We surrender." To her he whispered, "I am the one who is sorry, my love. I could not let them harm you."

As the lieutenant bawled an order and the cavalrymen closed in, Zach put an arm around Lou and she burst into tears.

Chapter Sixteen

The sun had set but Shakespeare McNair and Blue Water Woman rode on in the gathering twilight. Every mile brought them that much closer to Fort Leavenworth.

It was Blue Water Woman whose sharp eyes narrowed and who announced, "There is a campfire ahead, Carcajou."

Shakespeare had been thinking about Zach King, about how he had helped raise the boy from a sprout into the full bloom of robust manhood. He had always known Zach had a temper. Always known Zach harbored a keen resentment toward whites in general because whites in general treated him with contempt and loathing for being a "breed." But he never reckoned on it coming to this.

Sure, there had been a few times when the boy couldn't take the bigotry and lashed out at his tormentors. But Zach never killed anyone over it. Proof, in Shakespeare's eyes, that the attack on the trading post was spurred by Zach's fondness for the Shoshones and not in any respect by his hatred for whites.

His wife's statement brought an end to Shakespeare's reflection, and he looked up. The fire was a short way off the trail. "It could be anyone," he remarked.

"It could be Grizzly Killer and Winona."

Twilight was fading to the ink of night. They needed to stop soon anyway, so Shakespeare slowed, and when he came to a convenient gap in the vegetation, he left the trail and cautiously approached the fire.

It didn't pay to be too hasty in the wilds. Once, many years ago, when he was new to the mountains and as green as grass, he and two other trappers had unwisely ridden toward a campfire thinking the camp was that of friends. Much too late they realized they had blundered on a Blood war party. He was the only one who made it out alive.

Shakespeare spied a familiar figure crouched by the fire, and grinned. "Hail the camp! We're friendly and we'd like to come on in if you don't mind."

"If you do not we will be considerably offended," Winona King replied.

Blue Water Woman laughed.

Shakespeare never had understood bigotry, himself. The plain and unalterable truth was that Indians were people in every sense of the word. They were human beings, not "savages," not "heathens," not "squaws," not "bucks." Just people. And as Blue Water Woman and Winona amply proved, they could be darned adorable, too.

Grinning, Shakespeare rode into the clearing. His grin promptly vanished. Swinging from the saddle, he dashed to Nate and hunkered. His friend was as pale as snow but smiled at him and tried to lift a hand to touch him.

"You old goat. About time you showed up."

Shakespeare lifted the blanket and saw the bandages and dried blood, and his mouth went dry. "What did you go and do? Cut yourself when you were sharpening that pigsticker of yours?"

"I wrestled a bear," Nate said weakly. "The bear lost."

Not by much, Shakespeare thought, and looked at the others. Winona and Evelyn wore masks of worry. Even Touch The Clouds, whose ruggedly handsome face was always as inscrutable as a boulder, betrayed his concern.

"How bad?" Shakespeare asked Winona.

"His back," she said.

Shakespeare turned to Nate. "May I?" When Nate nodded, Shakespeare eased Nate off the saddle far enough to carefully pry at the bandages. When he saw the wounds, his stomach did flip-flops. He almost blurted out loud, "Dear God," and bit his lower lip.

"Is it as awful as they keep telling me?" Nate asked.

"I've seen worse," Shakespeare said. And he had. But not many who lived with cuts as deep as these.

"I want to head out at first light but Winona won't let me," Nate mentioned. "I asked her to go on ahead but she won't leave me." Again he tried to put a hand on Shakespeare's arm but couldn't. "Talk to her for me, will you?"

"You bet I will, Horatio," Shakespeare said, and motioning to Winona and Blue Water Woman, he walked off out of Nate's hearing and bluntly declared, "If he tries to ride out of here, hit him over the head with a tree limb."

"He does not realize how serious it is," Winona said, downcast. "Too much movement could kill him."

"Tell me how it happened," Shakespeare said, and after she had related the details, he stared at the hide Touch The Clouds had hung on a makeshift rack, and sighed. "I don't know what it is about your husband and bears. In the early days, he couldn't turn around without tripping over a griz."

"Grizzly Killer is rightly named," Blue Water Woman said.

"In the reproof of chance lies the true proof of men," Shakespeare quoted, "but it might be better for him if he were called Dandelion Killer. I'll go try to talk some sense into that thick noggin of his."

"You are a fine one to talk about thick heads," was Blue Water Woman's rejoinder.

"Why, how now, dame? Whence grows this insolence?" Clucking at her, Shakespeare walked over to Nate, and squatted. "We've hashed it out and come to an agreement."

"I knew I could count on you."

"A friend isn't a friend if he doesn't do what's best for the friendship."

Nate smiled wanly. "I told her I'm not as bad off as she thinks."

"No,'tis not so deep as a well, nor so wide as a churchdoor; but 'tis enough, 'twill suffice," Shakespeare quoted.

"You'll help me on my horse in the morning?"

"Certainly. Right after breaking both of your legs."

"But you just said—"

"What's best for the friendship, Horatio, is that you not move so much as a muscle for at least a week, and not stir from this clearing for two to three more. You couldn't ride a mile in your condition."

"And what about Zach?" Nate demanded, anger lending him the strength to sit straighter. "Am I to lie here while a noose is put around my son's neck and the life is strangled out of him? No, by God!"

"What good can you do him dead?"

"I don't care how hurt I am, nothing is keeping me from my son."

"We're not always masters of our own destinies," Shakespeare pointed out. He accepted a cup of coffee Blue Water Woman had brought him.

"Zach needs me."

"He needs someone, I won't dispute that, but it won't be you and it can't be Winona because she must look after you and it can't be Touch The Clouds because he must look after the both of you, so that leaves Blue Water Woman and yours truly."

"I'm his father."

"And the sun is yellow and grass is green and if disappointments were gold we would all be rich." Shakespeare sipped from the hot tin cup.

Nate groaned. "If they hang him, they might as well hang me."

"It's not like you to think only of yourself. Did you forget Winona and Evelyn? They care for him, too. Or do you plan to make it a family hanging?"

"Go to hell."

"Come, come, thou art as hot a Jack in thy mood as any in Italy, and as soon moved to be moody, and as soon moody to be moved."

"The Bard can go to hell, too."

Shakespeare decided not to mince words. "Whining and pouting like a five-year-old doesn't become you and insults those who care for you. But if it will make you feel any better, I'll start for hell tomorrow. Or Fort Leavenworth. Whichever you prefer."

Nate hung his head and closed his eyes.

"Fort Leavenworth it is, then."

"I am going too," Blue Water Woman said, and went to be with Winona and the others.

It tore at Shakespeare's heartstrings to see the anguish contorting Nate's face. Placing a hand on his friend's arm, he said more gently, "You need to keep your spirits up. You'll mend faster if you do."

"You're asking the impossible. I would be better off if the bear had killed me."

"Now you're just being silly. I'll come back and talk to you when you're behaving like the Nate King I've known and admired for twenty years." Shakespeare started to rise.

"Stay," Nate said. "Please."

"No more sniveling?"

"I'm sorry. I'm so worried, I'm not thinking straight." Nate gazed yearningly to the east. "I keep thinking of all the good times Zach and I had when he was growing up. The hunting trips. Fishing in the lake. The first time he rode a horse. Teaching him to shoot."

"You've been as fine a father as any son could ask for," Shakespeare commented.

"Have I? Maybe if I had done something different, maybe if I had been a shade better, Zach wouldn't be in the fix he's in."

"Whoa, there, hoss. Let's get a few things straight. There is only so much a parent can do for a child. You've done all anyone could expect, and then some. But you can't make their decisions for them once they're full grown. It was Zach's idea to wipe out the traders, not yours."

"If only I had been there—" Nate began.

"If, if, if. Hellfire, son, crying over what might have been is like closing the corral gate after all the horses have run off."

They were quiet a while. Shakespeare sipped his coffee, Nate was slumped in misery. In the past Shakespeare often joked that he had a quote for every occasion but this was one occasion when his remarkable memory failed him. He couldn't think of anything he could say that would ease Nate's grief. Some sorrows were unshakable.

Thankfully, Evelyn chose that moment to join them. "Pa, I wanted you to know. I've talked it over with Ma and she says I can go with Uncle Shakespeare and Blue Water Woman if it's all right by you."

With visible effort Nate managed to smile. "It's sweet of you but you would slow them down."

"Not that much," Evelyn said.

"A couple of hours can make all the difference," Nate said. "With your brother's life at stake we can't take the chance of them arriving too late."

Evelyn looked to Shakespeare. He pretended to be interested in the Big Dipper to give himself a minute to choose how best to respond. "Your father has a point, Blue Flower." He used her Shoshone name. "Too bad, though. Zach would probably like to have one of you there." When Nate didn't take the bait, he added, "I know I would if I were in his moccasins. He must be so down in the doldrums by now that the sight of a friendly face would cheer him like nothing else could."

Nate chewed on his lip.

"Zach and you have been as close as a brother and sister can be," Shakespeare said, pressing his point home. "You spatted a lot when you were little, but kids have a knack for clawing at each other like cats and dogs until they're old enough to know better."

Now Nate was staring thoughtfully at Evelyn.

Shakespeare rumpled her hair and said, "I dare say you're one of the five or six people he loves the most in this world. So don't worry. When I get there I'll relay word of how much you miss him, and how much you wished you could be at the trial."

"Maybe she should go," Nate suggested.

"And have her slow us down like you said?" Shakespeare feigned surprise. "No, it's better if she stays with you."

"Zach needs one of us there and it's a cinch it can't be me. I want you to take her and I won't take no for an answer."

"If you insist."

"I do."

Shakespeare raised his cup to his lips to hide his grin. "Fathers always know best," he said, and winked at Evelyn. She giggled and hugged him, then scooted over to where the women were seated.

"Just so you know," Nate said, "when I mend, I aim to throw you in the lake by my cabin and hold you under until you turn blue."

"What did I do?" Shakespeare innocently responded.

"What haven't you done?" was Nate's rebuttal. His smile faded and he crooked a finger for Shakespeare to lean closer. "Can you guess what I'm about to ask?"

"To be, or not to be, that is the question: Whether 'tis nobler in the mind to suffer the slings and arrows of outrageous fortune, or to take arms against a sea of troubles, and by opposing, end them."

"Will you do it, if it comes to that?"

Shakespeare was a while answering. "Your lordship's a goodly villain. The devil knew not what he did when he made man."

Nate's eyes bored into him. "Yes or no?"

"Boy, thou hast locked thyself into my grace, and art mine own." Shakespeare spread his hands. "To be honest, I would rather stick my head in the mouth of a starving griz than bait an eagle in its nest, but when the eagle is in the wrong, its wings need to be clipped."

"So you will?"

"Yes, yes, a thousand times yes. But I hope you realize what you're asking of me. I figured I had another five or six years left before the wick burned low. And my wife is liable to have a fit."

Nate placed his hand on Shakespeare's arm and tried to speak.

"There's no need to thank me. You would do the same for me if it were my boy. I only hope I don't let you down."

"You never have."

"Damn this life, anyhow."

Later, when they turned in, Shakespeare found sleep elusive. The gravity of the deed he was contemplating had fully sunk in, and he tossed and turned, aflutter with raw nerves. But the next morning as he rode on down the trail with Blue Water Woman and Evelyn at his side, he was his old self again. He had given his word and he would abide by it.

Even if it got him killed.

Chapter Seventeen

From the outset, Stanley P. Dagget could tell that the trial proceedings were rigged.

Judge Hardesty called the Federal district court to order and after a few preliminaries, jury selection began. Stanley was provided with a list of the names of potential jurors.

He was surprised when Arthur Hunnicut asked but a few trifling questions of the first one. Ordinarily, attorneys quizzed prospective jurors at length to determine which were favorably disposed toward their clients.

Stanley's turn was next. His hands clasped behind his back, he walked to the witness stand. "Your name is Samuel Varner and you are a farmer, is that correct?"

"Yes, sir," the fifty-four-year-old Varner replied.

"Have you ever had any dealings with Indians, Mr. Varner?"

"Personal-like? No sir. I mean, I've seen Indians here and there but I ain't never had cause to talk to them or anything like that."

"How do you feel about Indians and those dubbed 'halfbreeds'?" Stanley inquired.

"Feel how?"

"Do you like them or hate them?"

Varner shrugged. "I can take 'em or leave 'em."

"You don't harbor any ill feelings?" Stanley pressed him. "And remember, you're under oath. If you bear any prejudice, you are legally obligated to inform me."

"Well, I suppose maybe I might have a few hard feelings. After all, it was a pack of redskins who killed my grandpa."

Stanley soon discovered that every juror on the list had lost a relative or a friend or an acquaintance to Indian depredations. The odds against all of them having done so were so astronomically high, he deduced that whoever compiled the jury list had done it on purpose.

Stanley went through the motions of questioning each and every one, and when it was over, he stood and declared, "Your honor, I respectfully move that the entire jury pool be dismissed on the grounds that they are biased against my client and incapable of rendering a fair and impartial verdict."

"Motion overruled," Judge Hardesty declared. "I will not have this trial delayed by petty stalling tactics."

Any lingering thoughts of fairness Stanley had, evaporated under the harsh rebuke. He had no choice but to work to seat the jurors he felt were least prejudiced.

Zach King sat quietly at the defense table the whole time, shackled hand and foot. Four soldiers stood at parade rest between the table and the seats for the public. The courtroom was packed to overflowing with spectators, a rare occurrence. But then, the trial had been touted to sensational heights by the press, and was the talk of the territory.

Hunnicut only challenged one of the jurors Stanley wanted. The judge promptly dismissed him so Stanley chose another, who turned out to be acceptable.

"I bet there isn't one of them who thinks I'm innocent," Zach commented, studying the men who were to determine his fate. He leaned back, his chains rattling.

Stanley shot to his feet. It struck him that he had committed a grievous oversight which he must immediately remedy. "Your honor, I would like to make a request of the court, with your indulgence."

"Make it brief, Mr. Dagget."

"It's not customary to have the accused in chains. I submit it predisposes the jury against him, and I respectfully request that they be removed while court is in session."

"Request denied. Your client has already tried to escape custody once. I won't risk a repeat of that attempt."

Crestfallen, Stanley sat back down.

"What else did you expect?" Zach asked. He twisted in his chair. "What I don't understand is why they let my wife go."

Stanley glanced over his shoulder at Louisa King, who was in the first row. She had heeded his advice and bought a suitable if plain dress and was sitting as demurely as a schoolmarm in church. He, too, was puzzled that no charges had been brought against her over the escape attempt. Against Zach, yes, but not Lou.

"Not that I'm complaining, mind you," Zach said. "I just hope she listens to me and doesn't try anything."

Stanley wondered if that were the answer. Maybe the government wanted her to try again, here in front of everyone, for the whole world to see. "I hope so too."

The prosecution's first witness was Colonel Templeton. Under questioning by Arthur Hunnicut, the colonel related how Phineas Borke had shown up at the fort one day to report that his brother and six other men had been massacred by Shoshones. Borke had a frontiersman with him by the name of Jacob Hyde who happened on the scene as the attack took place. Templeton then decided to send a patrol to investigate.

"Your witness," Arthur said, wearing that smug smile of his.

Stanley paced back and forth in front of his table, as was his habit. "Tell me, Colonel. Isn't it customary for those venturing into the wilderness to stop at Fort Leavenworth and apprise the army of the fact?"

"Yes. Wagon masters do it as a matter of course. So does just about everyone else. It's a precaution in case someone goes missing."

"But you mentioned that Artemis Borke didn't stop beforehand, did he? Here he was, about to establish a trading post in the heart of Indian country, and he didn't see fit to let the army know. Don't you find that a bit strange?"

"Yes, frankly, I do," Colonel Templeton said. "I asked his brother about it but his brother never answered me."

"Suggesting, perhaps, a sinister motive?" Stanley said.

"Objection." Arthur Hunnicut shot to his feet. "The defense is engaging in rank speculation."

"Objection sustained," Judge Hardesty ruled.

When Stanley sat down, Arthur had one more question for Templeton.

"Isn't it true, Colonel, that a lot of people traveling west don't bother to report to the post? Mountain men and the like, for instance, who can't be bothered?"

"That is true, yes."

"So it's not all that unusual, as the defense suggested, for Artemis Borke to have neglected to inform you?"

"I still find it strange, but you're right, it's not all that unusual."

Arthur grinned at Stanley and took his seat.

The next witness was Lieutenant Phillip J. Pickforth. He sat tall and straight in a crisp, clean uniform, and recounted his patrol's trek across the plains to the Rockies. Hunnicut had him go into explicit detail about his investigation; how Pickforth visited the trading post site and saw the charred remains for himself; how Pickforth visited the nearest Shoshone encampment and spoke with their leader, Touch The Clouds; how Phineas Borke became convinced he was not going to take Zach King into custody so Borke kidnapped Louisa King to lure her husband into an ambush; and how, after Pickforth took Borke into custody for the kidnapping, Zach King then murdered Borke and was subsequently captured.

Stanley's turn came.

"You told this court, Lieutenant, that Touch The Clouds, the Shoshone chief, informed you the traders had deceived and cheated the Shoshones, and even gone so far as to incite the Crows against them?"

"That was their version of events, yes."

"And if true, it would explain the drastic steps they took, would it not?"

Arthur was on his feet again. "Objection, your honor. The defense is misleading the witness into offering personal speculation."

"Sustained."

And so it went, with Hunnicut challenging Stanley

again and again on trifling legal points, and Judge Hardesty always siding with Hunnicut.

Stanley refused to be intimidated. He asked question after question, patiently building his case. "Now then, Lieutenant Pickforth," he said at one point, "in your estimation, was Louisa King in peril of her life when Phineas Borke abducted her?"

Predictably, Arthur rose. "Objection. Once again counsel is asking the witness to make a supposition unsupported by the evidence."

"Overruled," Judge Hardesty said.

Both Stanley and Hunnicut glanced at the bench and said "What?" at the same time.

"Are you hard of hearing, gentleman? The prosecution is overruled. You may proceed, Mr. Dagget."

Stanley was so flabbergasted that it took him a good thirty seconds to collect his wits. "I repeat, Lieutenant Pickforth, was Zachary King's wife in danger of her life?"

"Borke threatened to kill her and I believe he would have, yes."

Facing the jury, Stanley said, "Show me a man anywhere in this land who wouldn't be in fear for his wife in a dire situation such as this. Show me a husband who wouldn't do all in his power to rescue her, and to deal with her kidnappers as they deserved to be dealt with."

Arthur sighed as he rose. "Your honor, the defense should save his oration for the summation. He's trying to sway the jury emotionally rather than adhere to the facts."

Judge Hardesty pointed a thick finger at Stanley. "Theatrics have no place in my courtroom, Mr. Dagget, as you are well aware."

"My apologies, your honor."

When it came time for Arthur to cross-examine Pickforth, he sought to lessen the impact of Stanley's ploy. "You've told the court, Lieutenant, that Mrs. King's life was at risk."

"Yes, sir."

"But you rescued her, did you not, and took Borke into custody?"

Lieutenant Pickforth nodded. "I intended to bring him back to face criminal charges."

"So Mrs. King was in no danger whatsoever when her husband snuck into your camp in the dead of night and murdered Borke in his tent, was she?"

"No, she was not."

Arthur's smile was dazzling. "I have no further questions for this witness at this time, your honor."

Next the prosecution called Sergeant Fiske and after him Corporal Bittles, two cavalrymen who had been on the patrol. They had nothing significant to add, and merely corroborated Pickforth's testimony.

Then came the moment Stanley had been waiting for, the moment when Arthur called Jacob Hyde to the witness stand. Hyde wore newly acquired buckskins and had cropped his gray hair and trimmed his gray beard to present the portrait of respectability. Under examination by Arthur, he told how he had been on his way to the trading post and stumbled on the massacre. How he had seen Zach King kill several of the white traders with his own eyes.

"So I reckoned I should do the right thing and looked up Artemis Borke's brother to tell him what I'd seen."

"You then went with the army patrol, did you not?" Arthur prompted.

Jacob Hyde told how he had offered to serve as guide, and said that everything went as he expected, except for a brief run-in with hostiles, until they reached the Rocky Mountains. "Phineas Borke was upset when the lieutenant talked to that Shoshone, Touch The Clouds. Somehow he got the notion the lieutenant wasn't going to do anything about the massacre, so he took it on himself to snatch the breed's wife."

"Objection!" Stanley exclaimed. "Please advise the witness to refrain from referring to my client in such derogatory terms."

"Sustained."

"Go on, Mr. Hyde," Arthur coaxed.

"Well, anyhow, it wasn't my idea. I tried my damnedest to talk him out of it. Phineas, though, was fit to be tied. He wanted to kill Zach King something awful. But it was King who got him."

"The details, if you please."

Stanley listened to Hyde impart how he and Borke had been placed in a tent, under guard, and how King had crept into camp right under the soldiers' noses, slipped into the tent, and slit Phineas Borke's throat. Zach tried to do the same to Hyde but had been interrupted.

When Arthur finally sat down, Stanley rose and went to the witness stand. "You experienced a harrowing ordeal, Mr. Hyde."

"I've been through worse."

"There are a few things I don't understand, however," Stanley said. "Discrepancies, if you will. Perhaps you could enlighten the court?"

Hyde nervously glanced at Hunnicut. "Anything I can do to help, sure."

"You've testified that after you saw the massacre, your first thought was to inform the brother of the man who operated the trading post, true?"

"It sure is. Anyone would have done the same."

"Indeed. But how is it, Mr. Hyde, that you knew Artemis Borke even had a brother, since, by your own admission, you had never been to the trading post before?"

Jacob Hyde's throat bobbed. "Well, I must have been there once but just misremembered."

"I see. And have you also misremembered the part you played in Louisa King's abduction?"

"I don't savvy."

"You've laid the blame at the feet of Phineas Borke, claiming the idea, and the execution of the deed, were entirely his."

"Yeah, so?" Hyde's nervousness was obvious to everyone.

"Then how do you explain the fact that when Lieutenant Pickforth and his men cornered Phineas Borke in the mountains and demanded he give himself up, that not only Borke, but you as well, opened fire on the troopers?"

"I didn't want to be thrown behind bars, is all. Besides, we gave up, didn't we? And later I helped the soldier boys track Zach King down. That ought to count for something."

"I'm glad you brought that up," Stanley said. "Isn't it true, Mr. Hyde, that you hold a long-standing grudge against the King family? That, in point of fact, Nate King once stopped you from beating your Indian wife at a rendezvous, and you've hated him ever since?" Stanley had Lou to thank for that interesting tidbit.

"Objection!" Arthur Hunnicut cried. "I fail to see how that is pertinent."

"Sustained," Judge Hardesty ruled.

Stanley smiled at the jury and returned to the defense table. Hopefully, he had planted seeds of doubt in their minds. If not, Zachary King's fate was sealed.

Chapter Eighteen

At Arthur Hunnicut's request, Judge Hardesty called for an hour recess. "We will reconvene at eleven A.M. sharp. I suggest those who are hungry find something to eat beforehand because I do not plan to call for a break at midday. We will continue proceedings straight through the afternoon, and barring unforeseen developments, I expect to hand the case to the jury for deliberation before the day is done."

Stanley was out of his chair before Hardesty could strike his gavel. "Your honor! The defense hopes to call several witnesses whose whereabouts are at present unknown. I planned to ask to be granted time to track them down."

"They have until the end of court today to appear," Hardesty said. "That is all the time I'll allow!"

Sinking into his chair, Stanley looked at Zach. "I'm sorry, Mr. King. They thwart me at every turn. Justice is being consumed by the flames of expediency."

"Which is your way of saying they're out to nail my hide to the wall and won't let anyone stand in their way."

"Judge Hardesty and Colonel Templeton both mentioned the army is out to make an object lesson of you," Stanley said, and rested his chin in his hand. "They're doing a thorough job of it, too, I'm sad to say."

"I can't help wonder if there's not more to this," Zach remarked.

"How do you mean?"

"Why this particular incident? There have been scores of clashes between whites and Indians the past few years. Fights where a lot more whites lost their lives than at the trading post. So why make a fuss over this one?"

"Perhaps it's the timing. Word is, emigrants will soon pour across the plains in droves. The government wants to reassure them that hostilities of this nature are being discouraged."

"Then why not take a case to trial that involves emigrants? Not that long ago a wagon train was nearly wiped out by renegades but the army never did a thing."

"If they're singling you out for some other reason, I'm at a loss to know what it is," Stanley said. But he had to admit Zach might have a point. "I could delve into it, given time, but time is the one thing Judge Hardesty is loathe to grant us."

"You're doing a fine job," Zach said. "I have no complaints." He rose. "Can you arrange for me to talk to Lou before we're called back to court?"

"I'll see what I can do." Stanley left his valise on the table and went down the hall in search of General Risher to ask permission. The general had sat directly behind the prosecution's table all morning, following the proceedings intently. But now Stanley didn't see Risher anywhere.

He had turned to go back when a door at the top of the

stairs opened and laughter floated down. It was the door
to the judge's private quarters, and the man laughing loud-
est was General Risher.

Stanley climbed to the second floor and looked both
ways. The hallway was empty. He went to rap on the
judge's door and heard voices, then more laughter.

"It couldn't be going any better!" General Risher declared. "And I couldn't be any more pleased."

"Just so you keep your promise and I'm chosen for an
appeals court bench in Washington, D.C.," Judge Hardesty said. "From there it's only a few short years and a
willing President to a seat on the Supreme Court."

"We never forget our friends. Nor our enemies."

Stanley again glanced both ways. The hall was still de-
serted. He held his fist poised to knock, but didn't. What
he was doing was unethical but he wanted to learn more
if he could.

"Just remember, General. Our deal holds no matter
what the jury decides. I can't control how the jurors
think."

"All we ask is that you continue to muzzle the defense,"
General Risher said. "You've done an excellent job so
far."

Who is this "we"? Stanley wondered. He would have
listened longer but just then he spotted Arthur Hunnicut
coming down the hall. To keep Hunnicut from guessing
that was eavesdropping, he rapped on the door.

Judge Hardesty, still in his robe, opened it, but only
halfway so Stanley couldn't see inside. "Yes?"

"Have you seen General Risher by any chance, your
honor? I would like to ask permission for my client to
talk with his wife."

"I haven't seen him, no," Hardesty lied. "If I do, I'll let him know you're looking for him."

"Thank you." Stanley turned to go down the stairs just as Arthur reached him.

"Well done this morning, Stan. You had Jacob Hyde sweating for a while, although what you hoped to prove eludes me."

"I do what I can, Art." Smiling, Stanley hurried down. His mind was awhirl with the implications of what he had overheard. Everything had been stacked against him from the start, deception piled on deception until his client didn't stand a chance of acquittal. It made him so mad he could hit something.

Stanley believed in the law. He believed in the principles of fairness and truth. And here he was, embroiled in a case in which fairness had been trampled and truth thrown out the window. *By God!* he thought. *I'm not going to stand still for it!*

When court reconvened, Judge Hardesty asked if the prosecution had more witnesses to present, and Arthur said no. "And you, Mr. Dagget?" Hardesty asked. "Have those witnesses for the defense arrived?"

"They have not, your honor," Stanley said, "but I would still like to call three people to the stand, starting with Mrs. Zachary King."

Lou did better than Stanley dared hope. She sat straight and prim, her hands folded in her lap, and answered his questions sincerely and openly. He had her go over the series of events from the time Lieutenant Pickforth arrived until Zach was captured, then focused on Pickforth and her belief that he had developed an improper interest in her.

"And what makes you so certain, Mrs. King, if he never came right out and professed his fondness for you?"

"A woman always knows," Louisa said.

Arthur had been taken aback by the line of questioning but now jumped up and bawled, "Objection, your honor! The defense is off on a tangent that leads we-know-not-where and has no relevance whatever."

"Sustained. Defense counsel's question and the witness's answer will be stricken from the record and the jury is instructed to forget them."

Stanley smiled. As every lawyer knew, whenever a judge told a jury not to dwell on something, they dwelled on it. It was basic human nature. He had planted another seed. "That will be all, Mrs. King. At this time the defense would like to call her husband, the defendant, Zachary King, to the stand."

Zach hobbled to the chair and sat down. He had combed his hair and washed his face, as Stanley had advised, and held his head high.

"In your own words, Mr. King," Stanley began, "I would like you to tell the court about the Ham's Fork Trading Post and the events that led up to the fight."

In a calm and matter-of-fact tone, Zach went over everything, from the arrival of the whites at Ham's Fork to the selling of liquor to the Indians despite a promise by Artemis Borke not to, to the subsequent attempts on the life of Touch The Clouds.

Arthur objected at every opportunity. Nine times out of ten Judge Hardesty sustained him. But Stanley forged on. He continued to ask probing questions, continued to elicit responses that showed the jury there was more to the case than the random act of a violent renegade.

Stanley saved his best for last. "That's about all, Mr. King. But before you step down, I have one last question." He faced the jury. "A lot has been made of the fact that my client is of mixed parentage. That he is a halfbreed. As if that alone were sufficient to explain his presumed rampage. But I ask you esteemed gentlemen of the jury to consider a fact that has been overlooked." Without looking at Zach, he said, "Mr. King, we all know that your mother is Shoshone and you are one half Indian. But what is your father?"

"A white man."

"And what does that make you? Half Indian and half—"

"White."

"Would you say that again for the benefit of any on the jury who might have missed it?"

"I am half white."

"White," Stanley stressed, and turned. "You may step down."

Judge Hardesty was frowning. "I still intend to wrap this up today, counselor, so if you have a third witness to call, I suggest you do so."

"Very well, your honor." Stanley walked to the defense table. "I would like to call to the stand General Terrence Risher."

Nearly all eyes swung toward the general. Whispering broke out, and Judge Hardesty pounded the gavel for silence.

As for Arthur Hunnicut, he nearly tripped over his own feet in his haste to rise. "Objection, your honor!"

"On what grounds?" Stanley asked.

Flustered, the best Arthur could do was say, "The general has absolutely no bearing on this case."

"I beg to differ, your honor," Stanley said to the judge, "and I trust you won't deny my client his basic right to defend himself to the fullest extent the law allows."

Now all eyes were on Hardesty, and he didn't like it. "Very well. You may proceed. But I warn you, counsel. If his testimony isn't relevant, you will be cited for contempt."

General Risher walked stiffly to the stand and was duly sworn in. He glared defiantly as Stanley approached.

"Please forgive my imposing on you, sir," Stanley said, "but would you tell this court where you are currently assigned?"

"Washington," Risher said curtly.

"That would be Washington, D.C., would it not? Our nation's capital?"

"Is there any other?"

The sarcastic reply drew a few laughs, and the judge smacked his gavel.

"So you are not assigned to Fort Leavenworth?" Stanley asked.

"I just said I wasn't."

"You came all the way from Washington for the express purpose of attending this trial, is that not so?"

"What of it?" General Risher guardedly asked.

"Oh, nothing. Nothing at all. Except one can't help but wonder why. To what end did the army need someone of your rank to be here?"

"This is a special case. A landmark, you might say. The army wants to ensure justice is done on behalf of those King butchered, and their families."

"You're saying, then, that the army believed Mr. King to be guilty before he ever came to trial?"

Arthur's screech rose to the ceiling. "Objection, your honor! Once again the defense is indulging in supposition."

"Am I, your honor?" Stanley was quick to say. "The general himself just referred to my client as a butcher."

More whispering erupted. Judge Hardesty had to bang the gavel a dozen times to restore order. "The objection is overruled," he said, but the look he bestowed on Stanley betrayed which side he favored.

"Thank you." Stanley glanced at the jury. They were hanging on every word. It was time to go for the jugular. "Now then, General. I remind you that you are under oath." He paused. "Isn't it true you were sent here to have Mr. King found guilty by any and all means necessary?"

"No," General Risher said.

"And isn't it also true that you arranged for the best lawyer in the territory to represent the prosecution and the lawyer with the worst record to represent Mr. King?"

"No."

"And isn't it further true that you promised the judge a judicial appointment in Washington if he would do all in his power to put a noose around Mr. King's neck?"

General Risher came half out of his chair but sat back down, his face a vivid red. "No, that is not true, damn you!"

Bedlam gripped the onlookers. Shouts were exchanged, and a few boos directed at the witness stand. The judge banged his gavel so furiously, he broke it, and had to take another from a drawer.

The moment order was restored, Stanley declared, "The

defense retracts its last question, your honor, and begs the court's indulgence."

"Indulgence, hell. The bench fines you one hundred dollars for contempt and another four hundred for your outrageous allegation. I should haul you up before the bar."

"Very well, your honor," Stanley said, knowing full well Hardesty would do no such thing. The judge couldn't risk a formal investigation.

Tension crackled as the summations were presented. Arthur's was brilliant, as always. He portrayed Zach King as a cold-blooded white-hater gone amok. "Justice demands that you find him guilty," he told the jury. "That you send a clear-cut message to others of his ilk. That you do your duty by your country and your race."

Then it was Stanley's turn. He stepped to the jury box, leaned on the rail, and smiled. "Did you hear my learned adversary? Since when does race determine a person's guilt? Yes, Mr. King is half Shoshone. He is also half white. But more than that, he is a man who has been wronged. Put yourself in his place. Would you stand by and do nothing while your relatives and friends were being murdered? Would you stand idle when your wife was kidnapped from your very home? I dare say you would not. And if *you* wouldn't, then how can you, in all fairness, find Zach King guility of doing what you yourselves would do?"

Stanley let them absorb that a few moments. "I know that each of you has lost someone to Indian deprivations. That's quite remarkable, when you think about it. So many of you on the same jury. And I know that when you think of those you lost, you burn inside for vengeance. That's only normal. So let us suppose for a moment that you went out and exacted your revenge. Should you then be hauled into court and hung? Is that right? Again, I say to you it is not. Again, I say that what is fair for you should also be fair for Zachary King. Look into your hearts, gentlemen, and be true to the principles on which our great country was founded. I urge you to find my client innocent of all charges. Not to condone what he has done, but to show to the entire world that America recognizes the basic right of all citizens to defend themselves and their loved ones, and that the fair and just rule of law reigns supreme in our courts."

There was a smattering of applause. Judge Hardesty sent the jury off to begin deliberations and adjourned the court. "We will reconvene when a verdict is reached." He slammed his gavel, glared at Stanley, and departed.

Zach King offered his hand, and as they shook, he remarked, "No matter what they decide, I have no complaints about how you handled yourself. No one could have done better." The soldiers led Zach off.

Stanley began gathering his papers. Only a few people were still in the courtroom and he didn't hear one of them step to the table.

"I was misinformed about you, Dagget. You're not the incompetent I was led to believe."

Stanley turned. "Why, General? At least grant me an explanation. Why in God's name put him through this hell?"

Risher's thin lips pinched together. "You'll never know. No one here will. But there is one thing you can be certain of."

"What's that?"

"Today you have made enemies in high places. Influential, powerful enemies. I'm only one of them." The general spun and walked briskly away.

Stanley took his time. He suddenly felt tired, so very tired, drained physically and emotionally. His valise felt five times heavier as he trudged down the hall and out into the bright afternoon sun. He was squinting at the sky, waiting for his eyes to adjust, when the door opened and the bailiff called his name. "Yes?"

"The jury has reached a verdict, sir."

"Already?" Stanley was stupefied. It had barely been fifteen minutes.

Many of the spectators were on the steps or lingering below, and as word spread, they streamed inside.

Stanley hurried to his table. Louisa was in the front row, and he smiled encouragement although the pit of his stomach was in a knot.

General Risher was conspicuous in his absence.

Soon Zach shuffled in, under guard, and shortly after him, Arthur Hunnicut arrived, nearly out of breath.

That left the judge. Hardesty claimed his seat with as much dignity as his bulk allowed, then rapped his gavel. "This trial is once again in session. Bailiff, if you would bring in the jury."

In they filed, as somber a bunch as Stanley ever set eyes on. He tried to read the verdict in their faces but couldn't.

As soon as they were seated, Judge Hardesty stared down at them. "Gentlemen of the jury, have you reached a verdict on the various charges against Zachary Raphael King?"

"We have, your honor," the jury foreman responded.

"Then will you rise and read your verdict to the court?"

The foreman stood. He unfolded the sheet, cleared his throat, and read loud and clear, "We, the jury, find the defendant not guilty on all counts."

Stanley P. Dagget heard a roar in his ears and realized it was his blood racing through his veins. He became aware of Zach King clapping him on the back, and of Louisa King embracing him and kissing him on the cheek. He was aware of laughter and the babble of voices.

A soldier undid the shackles. Lou leaped into Zach's arms and he spun her around in glee.

It was then that Stanley noticed someone over in the shadows, glaring raw hate at the young couple. General Risher was there, after all, and it occurred to Stanley that the Kings were celebrating prematurely.

This wasn't the end.

It was the beginning.

WILDERNESS

Fang & Claw
David Thompson

To survive in the untamed wilderness a man needs all the friends he can get. No one can battle the continual dangers on his own. Even a fearless frontiersman like Nate King needs help now and then and he's always ready to give it when it's needed. So when an elderly Shoshone warrior comes to Nate asking for help, Nate agrees to lend a hand. The old warrior knows he doesn't have long to live and he wants to die in the remote canyon where his true love was killed many years before, slain by a giant bear straight out of Shoshone myth. No Shoshone will dare accompany the old warrior, so he and Nate will brave the dreaded canyon alone. And as Nate soon learns the hard way, some legends are far better left undisturbed.

___4862-0 $3.99 US/$4.99 CAN

Dorchester Publishing Co., Inc.
P.O. Box 6640
Wayne, PA 19087-8640

Please add $2.50 for shipping and handling for the first book and $.75 for each book thereafter. NY, NYC, and PA residents, please add appropriate sales tax. No cash, stamps, or C.O.D.s. All orders shipped within 6 weeks via postal service book rate. Canadian orders require $2.50 extra postage and must be paid in U.S. dollars through a U.S. banking facility.

Name_____
Address_____
City_____ State_____ Zip_____
I have enclosed $ _____ in payment for the checked book(s).
Payment <u>must</u> accompany all orders. ❏ Please send a free catalog.
CHECK OUT OUR WEBSITE! www.dorchesterpub.com

LANCASTER'S ORPHANS
Robert J. Randisi

It certainly isn't what Lancaster had expected. When he rode into Council Bluffs, he thought he would just stop at the bar for a beer. How could he know he'd ride right into the middle of a lynching? Lancaster can't let an innocent man be hanged, but when the smoke clears and the lynching stops, a bystander lies dying on the ground, caught in the crossfire. With his last breath he asks Lancaster to take care of the people who had been depending on him—a wagon train filled with women and children on their way to California!

MIRACLE
OF THE
JACAL
ROBERT J. RANDISI

Elfego Baca is a young lawman—but he already has a reputation. He is known to be good with a gun. Very good. And he is known to never back down, especially if he is fighting for something he believes in. This reputation has spread far and wide throughout his home territory of New Mexico. Sometimes it works in his favor, sometimes it works against him. But there will come a day when his reputation will not only be tested, but expanded—a day when young Elfego will have to prove just how good with a gun he really is . . . and how brave. It will be a day when he will have to do the impossible and live through it. For a long time afterward, people will still be talking about the miracle of the *jacal*.

___4923-6 $4.99 US/$5.99 CAN

RAIDERS OF THE WESTERN & ATLANTIC

TIM CHAMPLIN

Young Josiah Waymeier, a private in the 2nd Ohio Volunteer Infantry, has been chosen to be part of a daring and dangerous plan. A select group of Union soldiers attempts to steal the *General* behind enemy lines and drive the engine straight to safety in Union territory, burning Confederate bridges as they go. Meanwhile, Josiah's mother intends to steal a shipment of gold bullion from the Confederacy and take it to a rendezvous with the *General*, to contribute the money to the Union cause. When the theft of the engine unleashes a desperate pursuit through Confederate territory, both mother and son find themselves racing not only to perform their missions, but for their very lives!